Praise for Mark Kurlansky

"Mark Kurlansky powerfully demonstrates the defining role food plays in history and culture.... A fascinating new book."

—*The Atlanta Journal-Constitution*

"Every once in a while a writer of particular skill takes a fresh, seemingly improbable idea and turns out a book of pure delight."

—David McCullough

"Fascinating stuff... [Kurlansky] has a keen eye for odd facts and natural detail."

—*The Wall Street Journal*

"Kurlansky continues to prove himself remarkably adept at taking a most unlikely candidate and telling its tale with epic grandeur."

—*Los Angeles Times Book Review*

"Brilliant ... Journalistic skills might be part of a writer's survival kit, but they infrequently prove to be the foundation for literary success, as they have here.... Kurlansky has a wonderful ear for the syntax and rhythm of the vernacular.... For all the seriousness of Kurlansky's cultural entanglements, it is nevertheless a delight to experience his sophisticated sense of play and, at times, his outright wicked sense of humor."

—*The New York Times Book Review*

Also by Mark Kurlansky

EDIBLE STORIES

| A Novel in Sixteen Parts |

MARK KURLANSKY

RIVERHEAD BOOKS
New York

RIVERHEAD BOOKS
Published by the Penguin Group
Penguin Group (USA) Inc.
375 Hudson Street, New York, New York 10014, USA
Penguin Group (Canada), 90 Eglinton Avenue East, Suite 700, Toronto,
Ontario M4P 2Y3, Canada (a division of Pearson Penguin Canada Inc.)
Penguin Books Ltd., 80 Strand, London WC2R 0RL, England
Penguin Group Ireland, 25 St. Stephen's Green, Dublin 2, Ireland
(a division of Penguin Books Ltd.)
Penguin Group (Australia), 250 Camberwell Road, Camberwell, Victoria 3124, Australia
(a division of Pearson Australia Group Pty. Ltd.)
Penguin Books India Pvt. Ltd., 11 Community Centre, Panchsheel Park,
New Delhi—110 017, India
Penguin Group (NZ), 67 Apollo Drive, Rosedale, North Shore 0632, New Zealand
(a division of Pearson New Zealand Ltd.)
Penguin Books (South Africa) (Pty.) Ltd., 24 Sturdee Avenue, Rosebank, Johannesburg 2196,
South Africa

Penguin Books Ltd., Registered Offices: 80 Strand, London WC2R 0RL, England

This is a work of fiction. Names, characters, places, and incidents either are the product of
the author's imagination or are used fictitiously, and any resemblance to actual persons,
living or dead, business establishments, events, or locales is entirely coincidental. The
publisher does not have any control over and does not assume any responsibility for
author or third-party websites or their content.

First Riverhead trade paperback edition: November 2010

Library of Congress Cataloging-in-Publication Data

Kurlansky, Mark.
    Edible stories : a novel in 16 parts / Mark Kurlansky.
        p. cm.
    ISBN 978-1-59448-488-9
    1. Food—Fiction.   2. Man-woman relationships—Fiction.   I. Title.
    PS3561.U65E35   2010
    813'.54—dc22

                                                            2010017475

PRINTED IN THE UNITED STATES OF AMERICA

10   9   8   7   6   5   4   3   2   1

To Marian, who loves her bulots,
Talia with her fresh grilled sardines, and
Tallulah and her chicken and rice

You see, it's sometimes a good thing for a man to take himself by the scruff of the neck and pull himself up, like a radish out of its bed . . .

—Ivan Turgenev, *Fathers and Sons*

CONTENTS

EDIBLE STORIES

RED SEA SALT

What could explain it, as he half stood, his left knee planted on the sidewalk, head turned down away from the rain, looking at the wet, dark, sparkling pavement, the leaves like soggy cornflakes, his right foot in the hole? His knee may have been stinging a little bit and his hands were spread like webbed feet.

He must have been heading somewhere, for some reason, and now he was standing in a hole in the sidewalk.

A pair of tweedy-looking trousers flapped past him with pressed cuffs darkened by wetness in the back. But nothing was said. Why was that? Wasn't this odd, to be standing in the rain with one foot in a hole in the sidewalk? Wasn't it against the named order of things? Or was he one of a thousand people stationed in strategically placed holes around the city for some purpose that he had forgotten?

He had forgotten a lot. Almost everything, it seemed. As he searched his memory he could find nothing except a sense that he once knew things and had forgotten fairly recently. Of course, it might have been years, but he had a sense that it had all been forgotten within the past few minutes. He was not sure if this qualified as a memory.

A warmly wrapped figure with the voice of an older woman—he remembered what older women sounded like?—walked toward him and said, "Oh! That's terrible. You have to try to be careful. These leaves get awfully slippery."

"You don't understand. My leg is in a hole in the sidewalk."

"Oh!" she repeated, never breaking her stride as she walked past. "That's terrible."

"Yes," he said without turning to watch her leave. "But don't you think it is also odd?"

Why was he here? Why did he stay? Why didn't he feel the need to pull himself out of the hole? It occurred to him that he might be staying because he had no idea where else to go. Still, he was in a hole. He pushed with his hands against the pavement to see if his instincts would cause him to spring out of the hole. The pavement felt cold—and very coarse. His hands hurt. He looked at them and found them to be wet and white with dark red crisscrossed cuts.

Someone was coming.

A pair of loose brown trousers, no socks, blue canvas shoes with hemp soles. The man bent down. It was a good face with deep blue eyes and red, deeply carved lines that changed color as the man talked—first pale, then red again.

"I'm not going to work tonight. Right? The hell with them."

The man was apparently drunk but as he leaned down very close, the man's breath on his face felt warm but had no smell of liquor.

"I mean the hell with them. I'm not going. Right?"

"Well, yes," he said, realizing that the man expected him to participate in this decision. "Right. Don't go."

The drunken man froze with his mouth open and then smiled and softly said, "Thank you very much," patted his shoulder, and walked in a crouch to the curb and sat down. "Want a cigarette?"

"Yes, thank you." He did? Then he must smoke. He remembered that. And having remembered something he felt much better and decided to pull himself out of the hole. It was only the one leg and it was only in to midthigh. It came out quite easily. But no shoe came with it. Had there been a shoe when it went into the hole or did he only have one shoe? He looked at the thin black sock. It was worn almost transparent at the heel.

Then a thought occurred to him. Maybe he too was a derelict, a drunk.

A derelict? A tramp? A vagrant? A bum? A homeless person? Would such a person use these words to describe himself?

He sat down beside the drunken man and took the cigarette he was holding out. "Bum" sounded better than "homeless." What word should he use? He stuck his toe through a hole in his sock. He wiggled his other toes, trying to free them also, but the opening was not big enough. Moving his toes across the sidewalk he could feel the metal rim of the hole where he had found himself. It was not large—about ten inches in diameter, which was too small for a manhole. Next to it were some wet, yellow leaves and a newspaper—a wet newspaper with the white turned translucent in the rain and pages of print showing through behind each other, creating a strange new alphabet.

That must have been what happened. He was a bum, was wandering around in his habitual drunken stupor, and had stepped on a newspaper that was covering the hole and his leg had fallen through. And then, with years of alcohol abuse behind him, he had simply passed out—and then woken up with no memory. A blackout. Isn't that what they called it? You see, he knew the language of alcoholism.

He tried to remember stepping on the paper, the surprising sensation of dropping into the hole, a second of confusion.

No. He could not remember any of this. But it must have

happened. He was making progress. At least he was starting to remember who he was. Or his condition anyway.

He watched the drunken man, the other homeless person,
light a match. He leaned toward it and stuck his cigarette in
the flame. He inhaled. The cigarette had no taste, as though
there was no tobacco in it. He sucked harder. He could feel an
itching sensation in the back of his throat. But that was all.

Maybe he didn't smoke after all. But don't all homeless drunks smoke? Maybe he had quit. Do homeless people quit smoking? But maybe it was before. He had quit
because it was bad for him. Then he had become a drunk.
Then wouldn't he start again? How would he know what
people normally did? He had no memory. How did he even
know smoking was bad for him? Had someone told him
and he remembered? Who had told him?

"Robert? Robert! What are you doing?"

He looked up and saw an unfamiliar woman wrapped
in supple, textured fabrics. He tried to look into her face
but he would have had to look almost straight up and the
rain forced his eyelids down.

"Why are you sitting there? Are you all right? Who is
this man?"

"I'm not going to work," the other man offered calmly as
an explanation.

"Robert, what are you doing here?"

I shouldn't be sitting here, he thought. Where should he

be? Was he supposed to be back in the hole? "I was in that hole," he said, pointing.

"Why? What happened?"

It seemed that there was no apparent reason for him to have been in the hole. He was glad. His right leg was starting to feel bruised.

"Did you fall in the hole? Are you all right? Where is your shoe? You're getting all wet, Robert. Where is your . . ."

"It's in the hole," he said with a smile, pleased to have deduced that, pleased to have an answer. He went to the hole and looked in. The tan leather instep of his shoe could be seen. The hole went straight for about three feet and then curved to the side and his shoe was sitting in the curve. Lying flat on the sidewalk with one shoulder pressed to the rim of the hole, his fingers stretching at the end of his arm, he felt the shoe between his fingers, grabbed it like a hungry lobster and pulled it out, and put it on his foot. It matched the other shoe. Perhaps he was not homeless. He stood up.

A surprisingly tall man, he found that he was more than a head taller than this woman, who, he had assumed judging by her legs, at least from his vantage point seated on the sidewalk, was a reasonably tall person herself.

She tried to rub the dirt off the front of his coat. "What a terrible thing to happen. I was waiting for you under the awning. Over there. I didn't see you. Then I saw you over there."

"Yes," said Robert. "What did you see me doing?"

"You were just sitting over there, Robert, with that man."

The man smiled sweetly. "I'm not going in. The hell with them."

She tried unsuccessfully to smile back.

"But what was I doing before that?"

"I don't know. That's when I saw you. What's the matter, Robert?"

"Nothing. Nothing. Where are we going now?"

"I don't know. Where do you want to go?"

Why doesn't this woman ever make it easy?

"I don't know. Why don't we go home?" He tried to catch the word and swallow it. He wanted to know if he had a home but as soon as he said it, it occurred to him that home might not be a place he liked. It might be a place he liked less than the hole. "Unless we have plans?"

"Plans?" She poked at his collar, an attempt to straighten it. Considering his general condition, the collar struck him as a strange choice. It irritated him, as though it reminded him of something irritating that he could not remember. "We were on our way to dinner, remember? Did you want to change first?"

Strange it had never occurred to him until now to see if he had any money. Or credit cards. Probably there was a wealth of information in his pocket including his name. He couldn't look while she was watching. It seemed he was on his way to a restaurant where he would be expected to pay and presumably the money for the food was in his pocket. Was there a lot of money in his pocket?

As they walked through the city streets he—Robert—studied everything for signs: the lights, the sounds, what people said. He was building a new body of memory and had already acquired one important piece of experience—if you wake up in a hole with no memory you become a fantastically observant person. He studied words, street signs, faces, paper in the gutter, the gutter.

Something was wrong with his relationship with things. Funny. Something was clearly wrong with his relationship with this woman also. She knew his name but he didn't know hers. But that was not bothering him for now. Something was not tying him to the world around him. It was as though he wasn't there—as though he were watching a movie. He remembered that he had seen movies though he could not recall a single one. This was like watching a movie from a very good seat. They passed a park but it didn't seem to have real grass—only green leafy imitations. Even the rain seemed false. It was wet. It was water. But was it rain?

Was the smoke from the vendor with the grilled meat really smoke? He walked into the thin white cloud and it burned his eyes a little and made him cough. But it still did not seem the way it should be—did not seem like real smoke. He thought he remembered something. It was

| 8 |

about smoke and grilled meat, how it really was, before. But the thought was gone now.

What was wrong? The grill, the sizzling meat, the smoke blowing in his face all seemed normal. This must have been the way it was before. But what had he almost remembered that wasn't here now?

"Don't tell me you want one of these kebabs, Robert," she said, once again trying to correct his stubborn collar.

He didn't? Why not?

"You hate them. You never eat things like that."

He did? Things like what? Why didn't he like them? How could you hate these little grilled meats? How could you feel anything for them?

"Robert, let's get out of the rain."

He had forgotten about the rain but now he realized that his shoulders were tense and his head lowered and his face wrinkled over his eyes because of the rain.

They turned into a building entrance and climbed one flight of stairs. The woman rumbled small objects against the leather insides of her purse. She was looking for a key. Was this her apartment? Or was it both of theirs? He moved his hands into his pants pockets noncommittally to see if he had any keys. He felt some in his right hand—two or three rough-edged metal objects. Keys to what?

The woman put her key into the door and turned it. She opened the door and walked in without waiting for him.

Since she didn't say good-bye he supposed he was to follow. The apartment had space. Long rooms with well-polished long tables and counters. The decor was spare. There were clean well-placed objects and a few large colorful pieces hanging on the walls—very large walls with no more than one piece per wall. There were places to sit also, not many but they too were well-placed and soft and comfortable looking. But there was something important missing. He didn't know what it was but without this thing, this apartment seemed almost not to exist. What was it? Or was it something that was missing in him? Something in him that was not there anymore. He felt a jolt from within and felt his body harden and he could not move. It had suddenly occurred to him that he might be dead.

Was that it? He had been walking along the sidewalk and fallen in a hole and died. Or maybe he died from something else. Maybe a heart attack. Maybe whatever you die from you wake up in a hole. Now he was in this strangely realistic afterlife. Strangely realistic? If it was realistic why was it strange? Just strange for an afterlife. But how could he say what an afterlife was supposed to be since he had never been dead before?

Who was this woman? Was she dead also? She had taken her coat off and thrown it on the back of a chair. Her clothes underneath were a little damp and closely fitting. Her hair looked hard; her head looked hard. Most of her was thin and hard but there were these occasional oases of flesh, islands of softness.

"This is for you, Robert," she said, almost triumphantly. She handed him a package of red crepe paper tied at the top with a curly silver ribbon.

Was he supposed to have a present for her? Was this some kind of holiday?

"Open it," she said in that coaxing way like calling over a puppy.

So he did. Inside was a plastic bag filled with tiny brick red crystals. The bag said "Alaea Sea Salt." Salt? Was this red stuff salt? He seemed to remember that salt was white.

"It's from Hawaii," she said. "Red sea salt."

He untwisted the metal twine holding it shut, took a pinch of the crystals, and put them on his tongue.

It was a mild salt, so subtle that he could not taste it. He could not remember exactly what salt tasted like.

"Aren't you going to change, Robert?"

Her hair was dark—darker because it was wet, he imagined—with tiny drops of water caught in the loose stray strands. Most of the hair was pulled tight against her head. It looked very severe but her brown eyes looked very soft. So did her lips. They were large lips. She didn't look dead.

"Yes. I should change my clothes. I am wet."

"Are you cold?"

He did not feel cold, but neither did he feel as warm as

she looked. The more he looked at her, the more he seemed to feel some kind of heat emanating from her body. He found the buttons on his coat and pushed them through the holes. Taking off his coat, he found another one underneath it, which he also took off. This did not feel exactly like changing clothes, in part because he had no idea where his other clothes were. But removing his clothes seemed good enough. He removed metal ornaments from the cuffs of his shirt. She was unzipping something.

She looked young. Midthirties. And how old was he? Old enough for her to look young. He was glad that he did not remember what he looked like. It was not important, and if he did remember he was bound to think it was. How nice it would be to never know. He decided he would also try not to find out his age.

She seemed to enjoy him looking at her and he went closer to her. Very close to her, his hands on her shoulders and his face on her face, he felt—disappointment. It did not seem to be as much as it looked like. Close to her, something was missing. But not everything.

She raised her chin and he put his face on her neck. It seemed warm and almost like real flesh. He inserted his face on her chest where her blouse was open. He heard something. It was her heart. He could feel her heart pumping. Her flesh was warm and her heart was beating. She was alive. He was sure of it. Putting his hands on the outsides of her breasts, he breathed softly on the smooth pale skin of her chest. She would now put her hands on the back of his head. He knew that she would. He remembered. He knew her fingers would move in slow circles on his scalp.

Yes.

He knew.

Yes. Her name was Margaret.

It was now morning. He was Robert. She was Margaret. It had been raining last night. Now it was not. Robert quickly sifted through his facts before turning to the day's questions. He had coped with yesterday's challenges fairly well, he felt. He thought he had even done well in that awkward moment with the red salt. But today would be more difficult.

He assumed he was supposed to get out of bed and get dressed and do something. Margaret was up. He heard her in the next room.

There was a mirror. Could he afford to turn his back on available information? He did not look. He found his clothes by intuition. Everything was where he expected it to be— even a wide rack of those strips of cloth that went knotted under the shirt collar. He had worn one yesterday though he was not sure why. He should wear one, at least until he remembered its function. He remembered how to knot it.

Margaret had made some tea. It was a rich orange color

and as he put it to his mouth, the steam wilted his face. The tea almost burned his lips. Surely he was alive. As he drank he could feel the heat moving down his body, though the tea seemed very weak and tasted like water.

"I'll leave with you," said Margaret. "Just let me brush my hair."

After last night, shouldn't there be something more between them? But Robert was becoming used to this sense that something was missing.

Outside, the sun was shining and everything looked brighter and truer in color. Without the rain, he felt free to look up and keep his eyes wide open. He decided it must be winter. A warm winter day. He felt neither the crispness and rotting scent of fall nor the fragrance of spring, nor the heavy air of summer. This was winter, although the temperature must be almost seventy degrees.

Margaret now turned to him and said, "Have a good day," kissed him efficiently, gave an annoying little tuck to his tie, and walked away.

"You have a good day too," Robert said, watching her walk away and, to his surprise, realizing as he watched her walk that he wanted her again. It might have been because sex with Margaret was the only activity he had found in which he knew what to do next. Or at least he thought he did. Margaret did not seem impressed.

Where was he supposed to go now? An entrance on his

right was marked "250." He looked in the glass door and saw a marble hallway with two elevators and a roster of names. Why had she left him here? On the other side of the street were a restaurant and several shops. Maybe he was to go to one of the shops. Or the restaurant? But they had seemed to deliberately choose this side of the street and she had stopped here—in front of "250." He walked in.

There were only four names: Ackerman Publishing; Bryant, Spender, and Locke; Amalgamated Enterprises; and Leland Industries. None of these names sounded familiar. He hoped that he was destined for Ackerman Publishing. At least he knew that they were publishers. Of course, he would be expected to know what they published. And then again, did he know anything about publishing? Not that he knew anything about anything else either.

"You look lost this morning, Robert." The man who said this simultaneously pushed the button by the elevator. The elevator door opened and he stepped in. Robert followed. The other man pushed the button that said "2." As the door was closing, another man stuck his arm in.

"Hi, Tom. Hi, Robert."

Tom and Robert said, "Hi."

When the elevator door opened again, Robert saw the words in large metal letters on the wall, "Bryant, Spender, and Locke."

What do they do? Robert wondered. He left the elevator

with Tom and the other man and they walked into a large room with many doors off of it. He tried to look like he was walking to a destination while he wandered into hallways wondering where to go. As he walked past people they said, "Morning, Robert," or "Hello, Robert." He seemed to be doing what he was supposed to do.

Robert realized that he still did not know his name. Was he Robert Bryant? Or Robert Spender? Or maybe R. Bryant Spender? Or just Robert Locke?

"Robert," he heard a voice say to his left. What was going to be expected of him? Could he pretend that he didn't hear the voice and walk away?

"Robert, I would like to talk to you for a minute. Can we go to your office?"

"Yes!" said Robert, much too abruptly. He turned and saw a white-haired man with gray, thin-lidded eyes. "Yes," he said more softly, "please," and made a gesture with his right hand. The other man led him to Robert's own office.

Suddenly a bell was heard by the elevator down the hall and the man said, "Listen, I've got to get some coffee before I die. I'll be back in a minute. Can I get you a Danish or something?"

"Coffee." He too wanted coffee before he died.

For the first time the man looked at him carefully, suspiciously. "You don't drink coffee."

"That's right. Never mind."

Now he was alone in his office, a room full of clues. But he had no time. The man would be coming back. He already was suspicious about the coffee.

It was a pleasant room, with a lot of open space around a large oak and steel desk. Yet it seemed so sterile.

Sterile? What did he mean by that? Everything seemed sterile. That was it. Maybe the thing that was missing was bacteria. Had they found a way to remove all the bacteria from the world? Or was it an accident? We are losing lots of species anyway. Now all the bacteria have become extinct. Frogs will be next. How did he feel about bacteria being extinct? It was certainly better than himself being dead.

There was no time. Everybody knew more than he did. Suppose he really was dead and everybody found out. But that was ridiculous. If he were dead, the chances were everyone already knew. Maybe that was what Gray Eyes wanted to talk about. Maybe he was going to test him. Walk in, close the door, and say, "Robert, who am I?" Or maybe he would close the door, tell him to sit down, and say, "Robert, we know you are dead and we want you to leave."

Robert looked out the door. The man was walking back carefully, on his tiptoes, his shoulders hunched forward, his curved, outstretched arm carrying a green striped paper cup with steam rising from it—coffee before he died.

Maybe he too had noticed the bacteria missing. Maybe that was what he wanted to discuss. Maybe.

Robert, feeling what he thought might be fear, moved to the safety of what he supposed was his desk and frantically opened drawers in search of clues.

"Can I come in?" The man closed the door behind him, not waiting for the invitation, and, leaning over, sipped his coffee with great earnestness. Then, suddenly looking up at Robert, he said, "Robert . . ."

Robert waited.

"As you know, Elaine is leaving in a few weeks." He sipped his coffee again. "And I want to do something appropriate. Something fun. You know, a little cake, a little champagne. Those little petit four things and—what do they call those little fruit tartlets?"

"Fruit tartlets?"

"Exactly." He bowed his head and sipped more coffee. Robert couldn't help thinking this was going to be easy. "Maybe asparagus, and little crab cakes and that tarragon sauce. And remember those little Chinese dumplings, the shrimp kreplach."

"Yes."

"Good . . . I think that's right . . . very . . . appropriate."

"Yes, dumplings are very appropriate."

"I think so too."

Robert was starting to think that he was good at this. "And maybe some of that red Hawaiian sea salt? I have some."

Gray Eyes stared at Robert. He shouldn't have risked this.

"No. That's a little too gourmet, don't you think?"

"Really?" Robert was genuinely surprised. Was that what Margaret was? A gourmet? Then he remembered himself. "Yeah, of course. Forget it."

But it was clear that it was already forgotten. "We all know about the leukemia, of course. But this is what we do when someone leaves and I think it is important to do this the same way."

"Yes, with the crab cakes."

"Exactly! Good. . . ." He leaned over his coffee cup and took a big, noisy swallow, sticking his upper lip straight out. He turned and as he opened the door he said, "God, this coffee keeps getting worse. Have you tried it today? Oh, you're a tea drinker. I forgot. Might switch myself. . . ." He walked out and closed the door.

Robert took out the bag of red sea salt, which he had brought in his suit pocket, hoping to find out how to use it. He was a tea drinker. Everybody seemed to know that. Was it important? Did it mean something? Was red sea salt used in tea? Why had she given it to him?

The meeting had gone well. Robert was confident that he had appeared to understand what the other man was talking about. It seemed very important to make people believe that he understood them. It might just be the whole key to getting by.

He was alone now and could search his office. It was clear that he was not Bryant, Spender, or Locke. The desk contained numerous documents and letters and even stationery with the name Robert Eggle. He did not care for that name. He reached in his pocket and took out the wallet he had transferred from his other pants in the morning. Yes, he was Eggle. Everything in his wallet said Eggle. He had six credit cards, which impressed him. He also had ninety-four dollars but could not remember if this was an important sum of money. He had a number of cigarette packs in his desk, so it seemed that he was a smoker. He put a cigarette in his mouth and lit it. He found it tasteless and disagreeable.

The woman whose desk was in front of his door ran into his office with a look of such horror that it seemed clear she had found out the truth about him—a truth, Robert supposed, that he too was about to have revealed to him. "You have completely forgotten," she said.

"Yes, I have," he said, nodding apologetically. She was staring at the cigarette. Not at him! He guessed. "I forgot that I had quit," he offered.

She laughed. "Just remember the building is smoke free now."

Smoke free? Was that it? Did it still have its bacteria? Was it just smoke free? "Don't forget," she said, "you have a lunch with Tim Hemming."

"I won't forget. Where is it?"

Now Robert discovered that there were a hundred ways to keep busy in this kind of office even with nothing to do. You walk to the coffee room and run into someone and chat—not for too long because you have things to do. Another chat in the coffee room. Another on the way back to the office for a rest. And an office was full of papers and folders to rearrange before the next coffee break. How could he have worked here and not drunk coffee? That must have been a mistake.

The minute he walked out of the building to go to lunch, Robert knew it was more than the smoke-free building that was odd. Was the outside smoke free too? It seemed—sterile.

He went to the restaurant and an energetic middle-aged man stood up in the back of the dark room and waved at him. Although the man seemed to recognize him, he introduced himself. "Tim Hemming."

"Robert Eggle." Robert winced at the sound of his own name. Surely he had once been accustomed to it and he could get used to it again. He hated the double "g."

"What do you drink, Bob?"

Why was he calling Robert "Bob"? Was that also his name? How did this Tim Hemming know that when no one else did, not even Margaret? He started thinking with nostalgia about his night with Margaret. "What are you drinking?"

"I'll have a glass of white wine."

"I'll have a scotch," Robert answered. This surprised him. He had planned to follow whatever Hemming ordered with, "I'll have the same." Robert thought he remembered something from before. Maybe it was just that he drank scotch but he thought it was something more.

The drinks arrived. Robert's scotch was amber and cool and smooth and mild and it poured down very easily. He drank several. Hemming sipped his single glass of wine. Hemming and the waiter both insisted that Robert order poached salmon and so it seemed the expedient thing to order. They kept saying it was wild but he assumed it would be dead.

The waiter then asked how he would like it "done." For a second he thought he was asking how to kill it, but that couldn't be. Like it done? Why were there always more questions? Why did he always have to reveal preferences? He was beginning to resent that. Maybe he had forgotten everything because he was fed up with having all of these preferences. Maybe there was too much information and the system got jammed. Or was he constantly being tested because everyone was suspicious and they were waiting for him to slip up—order the wrong drink, have his salmon not wild or done the wrong way? He had to try something. "Do you have any red sea salt?"

"Red sea . . . I'm sorry, I can ask but I don't think so."

It occurred to Robert that he could take the bag out of his pocket and save the day, but instinct told him not to do it. Gray Eyes had said it was "too gourmet" and he had said it in a way that made it clear that it was not good to be too gourmet.

The fish arrived off the grill, charred and spitting and hissing. But when Robert tasted the salmon, breaking away a flake with his fork, it seemed without flavor. Was it stale? No, stale fish is anything but tasteless. Was it because it was wild? In truth, that subtle taste of the red sea salt might be just the thing, but he'd better leave the bag in his pocket.

Robert and Tim seemed comfortable with each other. They drank and laughed and drank some more. Tim even had a second glass of wine. Robert was feeling warmly toward this man and wondered if he should confide in him. After all, this man knew him well enough to know that his middle name was Bob. Yet he had introduced himself.

"I guess we ought to be serious a minute, Bob. We have to say something to justify the expense accounts."

"All right," said Robert, who was growing accustomed to understanding only a third of every statement.

"I don't see any serious snags and I think we'd like to go ahead and move on this thing. What do you think?"

"I think it sounds good," said Robert. Oh, he was good.

Not twenty-four hours out of the hole and he could hold his own.

"Do you see any problems?"

"Oh, the usual," Robert said happily. "Nothing we can't handle."

"That's right," said Tim Hemming. Then his voice shifted. "I don't mean company problems. I know about your people and you know about mine. But I think it's important for us to be together on this, Bob. You and me. I think we have each other's trust. So just go ahead. I mean really think about this. I'd just like to pick your brains a minute. What do you really think?"

Robert lifted his empty glass and sucked on an ice cube—cold, but without taste. Putting down the empty glass, he reached for a fresh drink already waiting for him. "Tim . . . let me try to put this simply." He paused a full thirty seconds. "I don't know if you've noticed but there is a deadness to everything these days."

"Of course I've noticed. Do you want to know what it is?"

"I certainly do. It's been driving me crazy. At first I thought it was me. But then I thought, 'I feel things . . . I drink . . . my eyes are hurting because it's getting too smoky in here.'"

"I know. They need to enforce the no-smoking rules."

"Really? Is that it? Smoke-free buildings?"

Tim laughed. "You have a point. No, Bob, it's not you. It's not me. It doesn't have anything to do with guys like us. There is something missing."

"Exactly, Tim. What is it? What's missing?"

"I'll tell you what's missing, Bob." He paused dramatically. "It's capital!"

"It is?"

"Yes. Capital. The flow of ready cash. Venture dinero. There is no life without it. And we can't do a thing about it. Just ride it out. It's the damn Federal Reserve!"

The Federal Reserve? Robert tried to remember what the Federal Reserve did. "Tim, do you think it's possible for someone or something to just remove all the bacteria and microbes from the earth? To just wipe them out?"

Tim moved his mouth as though he were going to speak but he made no sound.

"I just think they are all gone," Robert explained.

Tim stared into a half-empty glass of wine, moving it in a circular pattern, splashing little waves along the side of the glass as though he had learned to do that in some wine club. "Not gone, Bob, just out of circulation."

"Bacteria?"

"Capital."

And soon lunch was over without Robert having learned

anything. Back in his office, he felt tired and, resting his head on his arms, he fell asleep at his desk.

There was a vibration. He opened his eyes. It was a noise—his telephone. He picked it up and heard a woman's voice saying, "Robert, your wife is on twenty-two."

He looked at the phone. There was a button marked "9322" and it was flashing an intrusive yellow light. "Thank you."

He put down the receiver. Who was his wife? Was it Margaret? He hoped it was, because his life would be much more complicated if it were someone else. And he had enjoyed his night with Margaret. Of course, he might enjoy a night with someone else also. He pressed the little plastic square.

"Hello," he said cheerfully.

"Robert, are you busy?" It was Margaret. There was something direct about Margaret that revealed a lack of romance, he thought.

"No. Not very."

"Listen, I was thinking we ought to go to Grover's for dinner. Make up for last night."

"Make up for last night?"

"For missing dinner."

"But I just ate lunch."

"Tonight, Robert."

"Of course, but . . ." He stopped. He had seen something that frightened him. He did not know why. It was the calendar on his desk.

"Robert, we were supposed to go out last night and you didn't want to."

"I thought I had a better idea." It was his first attempt at humor. He sensed that it had failed. He had to get off the phone and the quickest path was to agree to dinner. "At Grover's."

"Yes, Grover's. Are you in the middle of something?"

"Yes, I am. I'll see you at seven."

"All right. Have a good day."

Margaret had a way of making that sound like his instructions. Today you are to have a good day.

The calendar was a rectangular pad. The top left corner showed the month of April. The right corner had the month of June. Below was the word "May" and the number "14." May fourteenth. How could it be May fourteenth? That is the middle of spring. There is a smell of fresh mud and honeysuckle and lilac. Today didn't have any of those smells.

A park would. There was a park near here. He remembered that. He had seen it just this morning. But he didn't remember the mud or the perfume. It wasn't May in the park. Everything was dead. Maybe he had not changed his calendar since last spring. He opened the door to his office.

The woman at the desk had her back to him. He did not know her name. "Hello," he called out unassertively.

She turned.

"Tell me, what is the date?"

"It's the fifteenth."

"I see. The fifteenth of May? I couldn't remember if I had changed the calendar today. It says May fourteenth."

"No. It's the fifteenth."

"I see." He turned into his office and from the doorway said, "May fifteenth."

"You should get a calendar watch."

A calendar watch? He looked on his wrist to see if he had a watch. He did, but no calendar.

Instead of another stroll to the coffee room he walked out of the building. Walking down the street toward the iron gates of the park, it seemed that it was warmer than he had noticed. The sky was a bright, glass blue. The park was thick with the sap green glow of new leaves. He hadn't noticed that before, maybe because it just didn't seem like it would be green out. There wasn't that feel to the air. The forsythias were bursting yellow, the plum trees magenta; the dogwoods blossomed white with blushes of pink and the lilacs drooped purple. It was all there, on trees, on bushes, in the grass, in the freshly turned dirt of flower beds. But—but what?

But they did not smell!

Nothing had any smell anymore! He grabbed a branch of lilacs and thrust his face into the blossoms, tiny purple petals dropping on his collar, and inhaled deeply. Nothing. He dropped to his knees and attacked a bed of tulips with his nose like the deadly beak of a hawk. Bright petals fell. He put iris petals in his mouth and tasted them. They had no taste. Drifting out of the park onto the city streets, he wandered the odorless springtime city for hours chasing vapor, smoke, blossoms. Sniffing. Nothing. Gone. Deserted. Barren.

Dead.

That evening at Grover's Robert enjoyed a delicately grained fish with a thick smooth sauce, followed by a soft and moist bird, filled with things that were alternately crunchy, chewy, and melting. The fish was accompanied by a chilled liquid, light in color, the second course with a garnet-colored drink that was room temperature. For dessert he had a white fluffy substance that evaporated in his mouth. It was served with small red juicy objects.

He frequently asked Margaret her opinion of one dish or another. She replied evasively, like a politician facing a hostile press—was that a memory from somewhere? She used words such as "tart," "subtle," "dry," "light," and—the cruelest blow—"perfumey." Robert replied as best he could with words such as "delightful," "pleasant," "surprising," "wonderful." At one point she described a green bean as "a bit dull."

Robert suggested adding some Hawaiian red sea salt. Margaret smiled softly—one of the rare soft looks he had seen from her. He felt encouraged.

"No, really. I have it in my pocket."

She smiled softly again and said, "Cute."

Cute? Robert thought as she reached across the table, not for a touch of affection, as he had imagined, but to straighten his tie. Why did that so irritate him? Something from the past?

He would be patient and enjoy this life while waiting for facts and memories and smells to return. He did not yet have enough facts to contemplate despair.

What was he supposed to use the salt for?

He spent his mornings and afternoons in his office, trying to remember. Between the sessions was lunch with various unknown people. In the evening was dinner with Margaret, dining or drinking or going to the theater or a concert and then snacking. On weekends they breakfasted and later picnicked and in the evening hosted dinners.

Margaret seemed happy. So did a man named John. Robert had the impression that he worked for this man. John was frequently calling him or stopping by his office to congratulate him on some accomplishment. Robert knew nothing of these triumphs, which were always said to have been achieved at a lunch. The Tim Hemming lunch had been the first achievement John had saluted but others followed. Apparently Robert was a great luncher, possibly even a professional luncher.

Despite the fact that he was still not able to remember what his job was, Robert came to feel successful at it. Details were all handled by the woman in front of his office, whose name he either remembered or heard—he wasn't sure which—was Louise.

Small traces of half memories appeared. One of the people he lunched with looked familiar. He remembered disliking a certain food store in his neighborhood. He had attended college once in a place with gray stone buildings and a great deal of snow. Margaret and he had traveled abroad in lush tropical places but also in high, sparkling mountains. He knew how to ski. He enjoyed swimming. He belonged to an athletic club but he could not remember which one. He had enjoyed sexual relations with women other than Margaret. He could not remember with whom nor if it was before or after their marriage. He didn't know when they were married. He was partial to the color green. He had once had a golden retriever.

But he could not remember how to smell, and taste seemed to have left him as well and he was growing tired of eating and drinking. He was also tired of watching other people eat and drink and tired of talking about eating and drinking and making plans to eat and drink. But he knew that these things were important. He was reprimanded for not eating and drinking at Elaine's party. And he noticed that Margaret became melancholy if he did not want to go to a restaurant or was unenthusiastic about a dinner party, ambivalent about a picnic, or indifferent about a special weekend breakfast. And yet, it also seemed that it was important not to be "too gourmet." Why had she given him the red salt?

A lack of enthusiasm for eating was threatening his entire way of life. No one else he knew had this condition and out of desperation he went to a doctor. The doctor prescribed no medicine but sent him to a second doctor, who attached wires to his head one afternoon and then sent him to another doctor. All of the doctors concluded that he had suffered "a shock." The psychiatrists said it was a psychological shock and the physicians said it was a physical shock. They all agreed that there were no "behavioral aberrations" and comforted him with words such as "aguesia," loss of taste, and "anosmia," loss of the sense of smell. But he was told that his senses might return.

"You mean they might not?"

"Frankly," said the doctor, "they probably will not. The odds are against it."

Robert was transformed by this information. He was no longer struggling to regain his life—to learn the forgotten realities. If taste and smell were not to return, his memory would probably not come back either and he would never know who Margaret was, why he married her, or why he worked for Bryant, Spender, or Locke. He had learned new realities and he would have to live with them. One new reality was that he was bored with eating, bored with all this interest in what to him was a biological function—simply the first step in the digestive process.

Margaret was beautiful. Yet Robert was beginning to detect a feeling in himself that was either resentment or disgust. He had this feeling about other people also. Most people that he knew. But he particularly had it toward Margaret. It would come upon him while looking at her across the table, her face distorted, her temples moving in and out, bulges and lumps appearing and disappearing against the hollows of her cheeks, faint grinding and crushing and slushing noises heard from within, a slickness appearing on the lips—constantly feeding more and more fuel to a fierce and nymphomaniacal digestive system, while he only desired modest portions of one or two items of varying temperature and texture, quickly consumed and then—like most things—forgotten.

One evening while seated on high stools in a long narrow room in front of a long counter, facing a mirror in which he could see himself and Margaret sipping amber fluid, Robert asked Margaret, "Why don't we do something? I'm tired of sitting here."

"Robert, it is eleven o'clock," Margaret said, trembling slightly. "We have been doing something. We are always doing things. It is just that you always seem to be bored, as though you weren't really here, as though you had no connection to us." She got off her stool and left.

At his office, Robert was no longer the success he had once been. He still met people for lunch but he tried to avoid eating or drinking and the strangers would seem uncomfortable and John did not congratulate him anymore. He had fewer and fewer of these midday rendezvous and in time he wasn't lunching at all. He stopped hearing from John.

He had nothing to do. He would often leave the office. Sometimes he would go home. Once he found Margaret at home looking pink and fleshy and naked with a man whose hair was disarranged and face looked completely confused. Robert left. He could not remember if this had happened before. Was it supposed to happen? He could not remember. He could not remember their marriage or a courtship or an agreement of any kind. Better to say nothing.

After that, their relationship rapidly disengaged. She was often out until early morning. Sometimes he would not see her for days. They rarely talked.

One morning John telephoned Robert in his office and asked if he would come to his office. Although Robert had no idea where John's office was, he agreed cheerfully. It is always easier to agree. He wandered the hallways and reception rooms of the office space for more than half an hour before Tom saw him, as Robert knew someone eventually would, and said, "Hi, Robert, what are you up to?"

"I have to see John. Want to come?"

"What for? Some kind of meeting?"

"Yeah, I think so. We better go." Tom led the way to a young man's desk and asked if John was in.

"Robert," the young man said, "what happened to you? You better get in there." Robert naively stepped in while Tom wisely retreated.

John seemed irritated, though it was clear that he had intended to seem friendly. He told Robert that they had to "trim the budget." He was the trim and would have to leave and was being offered various packages of money—they were paying him to leave!

After that Robert passed much of his time at home. He seldom saw Margaret there. They no longer went places together and rarely entertained. When friends did come over they barely spoke to Robert. Apparently they were not his friends. They were Margaret's. Where, he wondered, were his friends?

Those few tentacles that had connected Robert to his life were relaxing, unraveling, sliding off of the things they had been desperately wrapped around—those few clues to his life.

He took nothing but the bag of red sea salt, certain that its purpose would one day be clear, and returned to the metal-rimmed hole. It was still open. No newspaper was covering it. He could no longer fall in it accidentally. But he could still place his leg in. He could step in. He could return. Start again. A hole in the sidewalk of a well-traveled street offered infinite possibilities.

The man in the loose trousers and canvas shoes walked up to Robert and said, "I'm not going to work tonight, right?"

Robert felt that he understood this man better than almost anyone he could remember. "No, you're not," he told him.

The man offered him a cigarette.

"No, thank you, I don't smoke."

The man waved him away in a gesture of disgust, just as others had when he didn't want to eat. "The hell with you. I'm not going to work anyway."

Robert carefully lowered his right leg into the hole. Margaret would not come by this time. Someone would. Something would happen. He was not dead.

He is alive.

His name is Robert.

HOT DOG

Emma and Howard made their way, hand in hand, down the vomitory and any one of the fifty-two thousand people present could have seen that they were in love.

It was a perfect amber afternoon in Yankee Stadium. They weren't talking baseball. Howard was talking about his new, big idea. Howard was about to put his successful gourmet food catalog, *The Food of the Month Club*, on the Internet. Emma thought Howard was a visionary, a kind of pioneer. Though personally she could not imagine buying food from a computer, Howard understood these things. He could see the future.

"Do you know what my most successful food-of-the-month offer was?"

"No. What was it?"

"All-time most successful?"

She didn't know but she was almost certain that he had only been doing this for three years.

"Two years ago. This Hawaiian sea salt. It was red. Two hundred people ordered it. How many do you think it would have been on the Internet?"

She was afraid he was going to make her guess but just then they were coming out on the other end of the tunnel and felt themselves being sucked into the excitement of a crowd, a baseball diamond, athletes throwing balls in a promise of great things to come. The thrill of September baseball is almost as difficult to explain to a novice as the reason why the tunnels into Yankee Stadium are called vomitories. That is what they are called and you don't challenge it because the Yankees have traditions.

Howard believed that there were only two perfect moments in life—a first night of love and walking into the stadium about to see a September baseball game. Now he had both, back-to-back, like a doubleheader. All his secretive imaginings of the different ways of having Emma, who he had to have, who he knew he would have, the ways he would touch her and see her and possess her, were still not as good as what finally happened.

And this troublesome team from Boston's final humiliation was going to be sweeter to watch than all his fantasies of it. September baseball was the culmination of the tempering of a chaotic spring and the refining of a long summer. In September, a soft new breeze added the urgency of fall to the lingering laziness of summer. A team could lose games in April, even in August. But in September every game had to be won. In September, the Yankees strutted like champions, like they owned the month, and the feisty Red Sox, like scrappy street kids with a lot of nerve and not much respect, were forever threatening to surprise everyone once down to their last chance. Worse, they never looked worried. They looked as though they were having fun.

Howard, a New Yorker, was having such thoughts as they approached the box where his season seats were located in row E, five rows behind the fence, just a few seats to the third-base side of home plate, one seat past the screen, within the tantalizingly dangerous range of foul balls.

But Emma, not a New Yorker, could not walk in front of fifty-two thousand people without wondering if they were looking at her. She was certain that all fifty-two thousand people were observing the evident fact that they had been having sex all night. It could not have been clearer. They both had darkened, moist, just-showered hair. He was wearing his Saturday go-to-the-ballpark clothes, while she was still wearing a Friday night dress. Pathetically obvious. But she didn't care because last night she realized that something she had given up hoping for had happened. It was just like she had thought it would be when she was eighteen, just like she had come to think it never would be—a sudden unshakable belief that life was poetic. So who cared what anyone else knew.

Howard was wearing his shiny blue rayon warm-up jacket with "Yankees" scripted across the front and a matching Yankees hat. Emma thought he looked like a little boy dressed in a bedtime outfit—he might have been Superman. It was Saturday's other side of Friday night's assertive, masterful lover. It was endearing when a man was both. She giggled to herself a little, looking at him in his Yankees outfit.

He had offered her a jacket to wear but she had to carefully confess to being a Red Sox fan—the first thorny issue in their new, near-perfect relationship. Up until then, she had been careful. She hadn't told him that she would never buy food from a computer, though she thought it. But this she had to be clear about.

But he didn't seem to mind. She thought he almost seemed to find it sexy, as if being a Red Sox fan—or, even wilder, sleeping with a Red Sox fan—was something a little kinky.

Looking at their tickets, the usher pointed at an enormous man, so large he appeared to be sitting in both of their seats. The usher, a small, thin woman, shrugged bony shoulders, apparently reasoning that the intruder was too large to evict. But Howard insisted. "I'm sorry, but these are our seats."

The man was a lumpy mass of flesh. His face, a microcosm of his body, was a series of tires and bulges—his real chin camouflaged by false ones, his small eyes squeezed between a multiplicity of cheeks. He stood up, more than a foot taller than Howard, three times as wide, Howard looking more than ever like a small boy in an outfit. Still, Emma noted, Howard was fearless and possessed of such confidence he had made this giant rise for him. He was in control and self-assured, as he had been the night before.

But the giant lifted a thick lumpy arm, like a huge ripe provolone cheese, and pointed around the box area. With a voice that was half gargle and a thick Bronx accent, he commanded, "Take another one. There's empty seats everywhere."

But Howard, Emma's Howard, unshakably held his ground. "They are season tickets. I always sit here."

"Today, not," said the giant with no particular emotion and he sat down, struggling to squeeze himself back between the metal arms of the seat.

Emma could see that Howard was not a man to be bullied. Calmly but with assurance in his voice he explained, "That's the whole point of a season ticket."

The giant no longer rewarded Howard with even a

glance. The announcer had started introducing the Red
Sox, one by one. The giant was watching, looking almost
studious. Why, Emma wondered, couldn't they just take
seats in front of him? That would be even closer. But when
she pointed this out, Howard said calmly, "Because these
are my seats."

Howard had two season seats. Emma wondered for
whom the other seat had been intended earlier in the season. Was this a regular thing? A night in bed and the next
day at the ball game? Howard, it seemed, was a man of
deeply entrenched habits. Was he inflexible? And if he was
that rigid, was he really a visionary? Were people really
going to buy food from computers one day? Could the
future be seen by a man who couldn't even sit in a different
seat at the ball game?

Defiantly, she took a seat one row down. She applauded
each Red Sox player loudly. Being closer than she had ever
sat, she could see the expressions on their faces, faces that
were so much younger and somehow larger and less bland
than she had ever realized. On this perfect day after that
perfect night, she quickly regained her feeling of content-
ment. Howard wasn't like that anyway. Howard would not
take the time to be a womanizer. He always had his own
schedule, his own program. He sat in the seat next to her.
She kissed him. He kissed back hastily. The announcer was
introducing the Yankees.

This was going to be a pitcher's duel—Martino Miranda for the Yankees and Blanky Barnes for the Sox. A few seasons earlier, Blanky Barnes had been the best pitcher in baseball. He had an assortment of fast and slow pitches that were unpredictable and often unhittable. Who could hit a ball that traveled ninety-four miles an hour straight for your head and at the last split second turned away and spun downward? Or a pitch that only traveled seventy-five miles per hour but looked like ninety-five and suddenly dove to the ground right in front of you? But of late it seemed many of his pitches were hittable, either because he was thirty-eight years old and less agile or perhaps just because enough batters had figured him out. They knew that when the ball was heading toward them it would turn away or when it seemed to go straight it was a slower pitch and would drop down at the last moment. If you knew the speed you could swing up as it was sinking and send it soaring into the outfield. If any team knew how to read Barnes, it would be the Yankees. He had pitched in New York for his six best seasons. They traded him when he started getting hit. The Sox picked him up for what they hoped would be a bargain price. But he was only a bargain if he got back his magic. His paycheck, his pride, his future—everything a thirty-eight-year-old pitcher has was in the balance on this perfect late summer afternoon. Yet Barnes could still saunter to the mound, ignore fifty-two thousand screaming New Yorkers, and look ready for a comfortable day's work.

Martino Miranda was twenty-six years old, only had three good pitches, and had been having his best season, striking out six or more batters a game. He was a young man still in possession of the delusion that he was unstoppable—still fresh enough to realize getting paid a large sum of money to do nothing but play his favorite childhood game was the world's best job.

The first three innings were scoreless, as, it seemed to Emma, Howard had expected them to be. He passed the time unpacking a shopping bag and spreading out his banquet on a tray he had brought. The tray seemed designed to rest on the blue-painted arms of a box seat at Yankee Stadium. He had Cajun shrimp, rolled stuffed breast of veal with pistachios, cold and thinly sliced, and cold artichokes in herbs and olive oil.

Rodney Wilson was batting for the Red Sox. Two outs. No one on base. Wilson was the best hitter the Sox had. Emma had often seen him hit balls over the center field wall at Fenway Park. A man of remarkable nerve and unshakable patience, he only hit one pitch and he waited for it. Sooner or later something would come belt high on the inside. It could be a knuckleball that wobbled over, a curve that bent there, a sinker that dropped there, or a ninety-eight-mile-per-hour fastball that flashed through.

Sooner or later a pitch would come to his spot and when it did, he would hit it with a level swing, not above or below, and the ball would shoot straight out like a bullet, all distance, only rising slightly and with speed and certainty, clearing the center field wall by inches for a home run. But what wasn't certain was if he could do it in Yankee Stadium, where the center field wall was almost ten feet farther away at that spot.

Miranda confidently snapped a pitch that slid just close enough to the batter to be a strike, but today he was putting too much movement on the ball so that it did really spin outside of the strike zone. He had thrown three balls and Wilson hadn't been fooled. Even at those speeds he knew the pitches would go outside and he did not swing. Emma thought at least one should have been a strike. "That umpire has too small a strike zone," she said to Howard, not complaining but just observing. Howard didn't seem concerned about the call and handed her a Cajun shrimp all orange with spicy powder that came off on her fingertips.

Did Miranda have the confidence to throw to the outside and risk ball four, ending his perfect game and walking the first Red Sox batter to first base? Or was he going to try to get by Wilson on the inside? Emma was sure that if he tried the inside, Wilson would hit it. That was the pitch he was waiting for. The only question was would it go far enough.

Emma loved these seats. She looked at Wilson, who, batting left-handed, was facing her. He was smiling! She looked at Miranda on the mound holding the ball as though it had a surprise inside it. Could he make Wilson pay for that smile? She looked at Howard; he was reading the label on a bottle of Italian white wine that he kept cool in an insulated metal sleeve.

Then she heard the plum-ripe thwack of the pitch in the catcher's mitt. She had missed it and looked up in confusion first at the umpire, then at the scoreboard.

It was a strike. Miranda, unafraid, must have found his outside strike. Then he did it again, just barely inside the strike zone on the outside corner.

It was now three balls and two strikes—one pitch left. Would Wilson swing? Or would he hope for a ball and walk to first base? Miranda would throw a strike. He had to because he knew this was not a batter who would swing at a ball. Could he keep it away from him? He didn't look worried. Wilson stood at the plate, calmly waiting for his pitch, on the inside, where he knew it would be.

The pitch smacked into the catcher's mitt at ninety-five miles an hour, high and to the outside. The umpire called a strike. Three outs for the Red Sox. The Yankees jogged off the field victoriously as Howard held the bottle toward Emma so she could see. "Veneto," he said.

Emma thought Howard an amazingly confident man.

He had never doubted that Miranda would get Wilson out. Miranda played at confidence but probably had his doubts, but not Howard.

She didn't really want all this food. She wanted beer, not wine, and she wanted a hot dog. She had always heard that Yankee Stadium had better hot dogs than Fenway Park and she wanted to find out if it was true or just more Yankees propaganda. Clearly New York had better hot dogs than Boston. They had taken to serving clam chowder at Fenway Park but Emma felt certain that you should eat hot dogs at the ballpark.

But she didn't want to hurt Howard, seated happily in his outfit, so she sipped her Venetian wine and nibbled on her spicy shrimp and smelled with longing the steam from the metal box of the nearby hot dog vendor. As she ate, she could see things coming unattractively out of the mouths of Red Sox players, sometimes lingering on the lips. What were they spitting? Were they some kind of seeds? She wondered if these seats were too close. Maybe baseball players were better seen from a distance.

Barnes, when he was throwing well, did not walk batters. He was the kind of pitcher that tricked batters into swinging at the air. Through three innings he had thrown strikes and balls, only a few hittable pitches, and no one had gotten on base. He was pitching the way he had thrown for the Yankees and the Yankees were striking out or popping out to the infield. Barnes's most hittable pitch was a high fastball, about ninety-eight miles per hour but straight through the strike zone. There were no tricks; the batter simply had to be fast enough.

Emma started to notice something.

Whenever Barnes threw his hittable fastball she would hear a strange sound from behind her. Just as the pitch approached the plate, the giant who was sitting in their seat would shout in his huge, throaty, gurgling voice, rhythmically annunciating the syllables like a three-note song, *"La-sa-gna!"*

It is well known that Major League Baseball players are highly disciplined professionals, conditioned not to be distracted by noisy spectators. Sitting no more than twenty feet from home plate, the batters could certainly hear the lasagna cry piercing the air like the sudden call of a crow. Could it stop them for just a fraction of a second, which was all it would take to miss a ninety-eight-mile-per-hour fastball? The only known fact was that every time Barnes threw his hittable fastball, the giant shouted, *"La-sa-gna!"* the last syllable slowly fading out as the bat found only air and the ball hit the mitt.

Emma looked over at Howard and saw him munching on his shrimp and veal and artichokes. She tried not to think about the olive oil on his fingers and his chin. It disturbed her much more than it should.

She supposed that it wasn't really the olive oil. What annoyed her was that Howard was absolutely certain that the Yankees would win. They all were. There was Blanky Barnes, throwing a perfect game. Through the fourth, fifth, and sixth innings the game was scoreless. Both Blanky Barnes and Martino Miranda were throwing perfect games—no hits, no walks, no errors: no batters ever getting on base. At least one of them would make a mistake, but for now both seemed to be flawlessly working their craft. By the end of the sixth Barnes had thrown ten strikeouts. Miranda, also with a perfect game, only had eight. And yet fifty-two thousand New Yorkers were absolutely certain that the Red Sox would lose and the Yankees would win as though that was the preordained way of nature. God, she hated Yankees fans—except for Howard, of course.

She was beginning to feel the haze on the day that came from no sleep. Objects blurred. It was hard to focus. Eyes and thoughts wandered. Now she was looking at Howard's socks. Howard was wearing white socks with little blue Yankees emblems embroidered on the tops.

She tried not to think about it.

Wilson was up again in the seventh inning. He was a Fenway Park specialist. He could hit a short, high fly barely clearing Fenway Park's close but high left field wall, the Green Monster. Wilson had other tricks. Emma had seen him in late innings in a close game in Boston hit a hard, straight line drive to an exact spot in the left field wall where there is a closed doorway. If he could get the ball to ricochet off the far door frame to the near side and back, it would so confound the left fielder that Wilson could make it to third base.

But what, Emma now wondered, could he do here in Yankee Stadium?

Then Miranda made a mistake. It was the worst thing he could have done. After missing two balls on the outside, though he thought they had been in, he tried a little more inside but instead it went way inside. As soon as the pitch passed his fingertips Wilson could see it was going inside and he was ready for it.

A crack like a gunshot in the woods sent the ball speeding toward the center field wall. As it approached, the Yankee center fielder leaped up, sticking his glove just above the wall exactly where the ball was headed, and Wilson was out—a few feet too soft for Yankee Stadium.

Howard sipped his wine unconcerned. He had known the center fielder would catch it. Wasn't he paid to catch the ball? There were only two moments in the game in which Howard seemed momentarily flustered. The first was in the eighth inning when Red Sox batter Tommy Delano hit a foul ball on a three-and-two count. The ball went into the stands and didn't count, but it was an important swing because it gave the Red Sox hitter another chance, forcing Miranda to pitch him again. The pitchers were getting tired and every pitch brought them closer to a fatal mistake. It was only a question of who tired faster. Miranda had age on his side. But the Red Sox, by nicking away at such pitches and sending them into the stands, had forced him to throw many more pitches than Barnes.

None of this concerned Howard. What worried him was that this foul ball was about to come smashing down on his picnic. At first Emma longed to see artichokes and veal slices flying but then she worried about the olive oil that was about to splash. As she tried to cover her dress with her arms, Howard, without standing up, held out both hands and caught the ball, as though he sat there catching balls every afternoon. The people in the surrounding seats applauded. But Howard was busy with other things. Two drops of wine had spilled on his blue Yankees jacket when he reached up. He tossed the ball to a small boy nearby, who gazed in amazement at the trophy while Howard blotted the wine spots with a cloth napkin.

Emma had thought that Howard would be a good father. But now she thought about how he hadn't even smiled at the boy, barely looked at him. He just wanted to be rid of the ball and to tend to his tray while Miranda struck out Delano on the next pitch, as Howard had seemed to know he would.

The other incident was in the ninth inning, and this was the one that Emma found more difficult to forgive.

The game was still scoreless and, unless a pitcher made a mistake or a batter pulled off a surprise, it was going to go into extra innings. The blue sky was darkening to navy around the Bronx County Courthouse. The lights were coming on in the stadium.

Which one of the pitchers was going to make a mistake first? Miranda looked tired, but Barnes looked exhausted. Some managers might have taken him out of the game but Jimmy Dutton of the Red Sox did not have the heart to rob him of the chance to resurrect his baseball career with nine perfect innings. His weary fingers were losing their grip. His weakening knees made it difficult to plant his feet. His slider wouldn't hit the strike zone anymore; his curve turned too far outside; his sinker sunk into the dirt. Faced with three balls and no strikes, he had to throw a strike and he had only one pitch left that he was certain he could get into the strike zone. Age always gets the legs first, not always the shoulder. He still had his fastball. It would hurt but he could do it.

Like a bullet it flew into the strike zone.

Then the cry was heard. *"La-sa-gna!"*

The batter missed. The giant raised his fist in the air and whispered as though imitating the hissy refrain of a crowd, "Yes."

Three balls and one strike. Emma could see in Barnes's face that he was going to do it again. It would be a mistake. No! she almost called out. He snapped it.

"La-sa-gna-a-a!" went the cry, the last syllable slowly fading out as the umpire called strike two.

Then Emma saw Howard looking perturbed for only the second time, turning and glaring at the lumpy giant as he raised his provolone arm and again hissed, "Yes."

It was a full count. Barnes could try for something with movement and probably destroy his perfect game with a walk or he could take a chance on the fastball. The batter would be expecting it but he might miss if the pitch was fast enough; and Barnes would throw it a little high, forcing the batter to swing up and with luck hit a pop-up and be caught out.

As Barnes was cranking up his shoulder, Howard was turning around with a Cajun shrimp in his hand.

"Excuse me. Care for a Cajun shrimp?"

The giant stared at Howard's greasy, pepper-reddened fingers as he heard a crack. The ball shot up so high it was hard to see and when it came down it was on the other side of the left field wall.

The Yankees won 1–0. Howard knew they would.

The voice of Frank Sinatra singing "New York, New York" sailed over the stadium as Barnes and the Red Sox, like wounded cats, limped away and vanished. The Yankees went onto the field, lining up to tap fists in their victory ritual.

Emma and Howard made their way through the vomitory. Howard had his arm around Emma. She thought she could smell the menacing nearness of his olive oil–smudged fingers. She longed to free her shoulder, to be back in her own apartment, her own bed, alone. Maybe she would pick up a hot dog on the way.

Howard had been right about some things. She saw that now. He had been right to insist on his own seats where he always sat. There were certain things you should insist on, never let change. One of them, Emma thought, was that when you go to a ball game, you eat hot dogs. And you never buy them from a computer but a man walking the aisles with a metal box full of steam. That was just the way it was supposed to be.

MUFFINS

After Big Biscuit collapsed dead in an enormous heap, photographed onstage looking like a larger-than-life melting mousse, Kugelman saw a number of reasons for suspicion. He always did. Then he doubted himself.

Yes, Kugelman's portfolio had grown. He had started with nothing, and now look at him, as they always said. But that was the trouble. He never really did look at himself. And when he stepped on the scale, drama rising with each tap of the sliding weights, he read 243 pounds, which seemed to be about fifty—maybe sixty—pounds more than last time he weighed himself, more than twenty years before. But why trust these scales?

Well, he was a big man. Everybody said that, and

Kugelman thought that about himself. But wasn't this exactly what had killed Big Biscuit?

Big Biscuit was a rap star. He was said to be the first Jewish rapper to sell a double platinum record, *Chew It!* Jewish Rapper: that was what first got Kugelman's attention. One morning, getting ready for work, he heard a radio commentator mention Big Biscuit, "the Jewish Rapper," and the phrase caught his hard-to-focus early morning attention. What, he wondered, is a Jewish wrapper? Then he realized Big Biscuit was a rapper (though if anything seemed less Jewish to him than a rap star, it was a biscuit).

Only a few days later, riding the subway downtown to work, he saw a picture on the back page of someone else's *Daily News*. Big Biscuit was a heavyset man, his face too bloated to guess at the age, let alone ethnicity. He was so wide, so uniformly round, he looked like something with too much yeast that had puffed up in the oven—Big Biscuit. Hanging in front of his black silk shirt was a gold necklace with a Star of David so large that it even looked large on him. Kugelman suspected something anti-Semitic. That was the way it was with Kugelman. He always wanted to know who were the Jews and who were the anti-Semites. Those were the only two kinds of people that interested him.

After Big Biscuit melted into a heap onstage, pictures of him ran in newspapers, in magazines, on television. If you want your passing to be noted, die onstage. Kugelman wondered if he had planned it. The reports said that Big Biscuit was twenty-seven years old, weighed 475 pounds, and had died from being too big. Maybe. Paranoia, Kugelman always said, was a good theory that lacked evidence.

Despite his suspicions that anti-Semites had somehow done in "our only rap artist," Kugelman, only 243 pounds himself, gave the official theory of Big Biscuit's cause of death enough credence to join a gym. Soon he was sweating on a treadmill. The gym in his neighborhood was called a club and tried hard not to look like a gym—it had lots of brushed steel and mirrors, more like a ship. There was even a café and snack bar on the ground floor.

Kugelman estimated that the membership was "about forty percent Jewish." That was acceptable. There was even a Jewish trainer, almost as rare as a Jewish rapper, though even Kugelman had to admit that he didn't look as fit as the gentile trainers. He was probably just hired to please the Jews, so he was proof that (a) they were not anti-Semites but philo-Semites, which is pretty much the same thing, and (b) there was a significant number of Jewish members to worry about.

This club seemed the right place because it was not frequented by perfectly trained, sinewy bodies, but by large Jewish people like himself—rows of overweight men and women sweating side by side while staring up at no fewer than sixteen television monitors, at least half of which offered financial news. Several of the other overweight Jewish members admitted that they too had been motivated by the death of Big Biscuit.

His initial goal was three ten-minute miles. The machine, which reported mileage, time, and calories burned, informed him after a successful run that he had burned 550 calories. Some days it was more. Even without the red glowing numbers on the treadmill, he could tell that he was burning calories because he was hungry. After three miles, he ached with hunger. Sometimes he got to 3.08 miles; once, as high as 3.14. The more he ran, the hungrier he became. This, of course, was the point of the snack bar on the ground floor. It sold a variety of no-calorie cold drinks and fat-free muffins.

Kugelman thought the muffins were one of the greatest foods he had ever tasted. There were carrot, bran, bran and raisin, poppy seed, lemon, almond, cranberry, chocolate chip, fudge, cinnamon walnut—limitless ideas for muffins. They were only sixty calories each. What would be the harm of even three muffins, 180 calories, after burning 570 calories? He thought about the muffins while he was enduring the pain of running. As he felt his middle cramping, a knee hurting, an ankle crying for rest, he would look at the screen on the machine and quickly calculate how many minutes were left until he would be sitting at one of the little round tables by the snack bar eating muffins. Today maybe he would try the orange, and there was blueberry....

And all this running was making Kugelman rich. He mounted his treadmill and plugged in his earphones, and as the belt started, while a message appeared on the machine instructing him to "have a good workout," he began to listen to  the television on several screens informing him of the fate of the Dow and the NASDAQ. The NASDAQ was always up. The Dow danced up and down around it like a courting mate. Then came the sectors. Technologies up, utilities down, financials wavering, pharmaceuticals rebounding. Not only were there the quarterly earnings but the projected quarterly earnings and the possible mergers and the new market developments and ...

There is an old Wall Street adage, "Sell on the rumor, buy on the fact." But Kugelman could see that the markets were being driven by rumors on television. He would get his half hour of rumors, then another half hour of muffins, and more rumors with the muffins (there was a television in the snack bar also). Then he would leave and call his broker and trade. No one at this gym was watching ball games or soap operas. They were all doing what Kugelman was doing. He would see them on the treadmills, at the muffin bar, and then on the sidewalk, cell phones in hand, trading.

Kugelman reasoned that if he knew all the rumors, he would know exactly when everyone else was selling and buying. It worked. He was making thousands.

And he liked the muffins.

He had completely recuperated the money he had lost on tobacco back when he had failed to pay attention to the rumors that they were deliberately addicting children to nicotine. Biotechs and pharmaceuticals were where he was making his money now. He had never even thought of biotechs before he started running.

Sometimes he thought of striking up a conversation with the other corpulent investors sitting around the muffin bar, but that didn't seem to be what was done. Those few brief comments on the fall of Big Biscuit were the longest conversations he had overheard at his new gym. A woman named Rogers wanted to talk to him. But she didn't know how to start it either. She wore black tights and leotards of bright colors—expensive, stylish workout wear. She felt that she looked good, though, of course, there was no hiding her bulges. But Kugelman bulged too; otherwise she never would have been able to start a conversation with him.

Kugelman had noticed her too. He liked the way she jiggled. One day she had an idea. She tripped and nearly fell onto his treadmill. He wanted to be gallant but a manager from the Shears Growth Fund was talking about Alcox, which Kugelman had bought several weeks earlier and which had already dropped ten points instead of climbing as he had imagined, and Kugelman was thinking of selling. He did not have time that particular second to notice a well-laid plot at his feet.

Then one day Kugelman stepped on the scales, fidgeted with the weights, and read, to his amazement, 253 pounds. How was this possible? He was running. Were the scales wrong? Did they rig the scales to keep you coming to the gym? Somewhere in this, Kugelman was certain, lay a conspiracy and it was probably an anti-Semitic one.

The NASDAQ stayed up; the Dow dipped and then rose. Biotechs and microchips were hot. Mergers were everywhere. And another 580 calories were burned. He was running a little more and a little faster.

While ordering a carrot raisin he noticed a heavyset man who had been next to him on the treadmill buying an apple muffin. Kugelman introduced himself. The man was named Jarvis. He wore a green T-shirt and khaki shorts and black leggings and looked like a huge, sweating praying mantis.

"I noticed that you have been running a lot," Kugelman began.

"Yeah," Jarvis sighed, crumpling into one of the chairs.

"Have you been losing weight?"

"Not really," he said with a mischievous smile.

"Me either," said Kugelman. He gathered up his muffin and sat at the same table. "Why do you think that is?"

Jarvis shrugged and pointed at the television screen. "Biotechs," he said. "They have a new invention a minute and they are going to dominate."

"Overpriced," said Rogers at the next table, wanting to join the conversation. Jarvis attacked, pointing out that some of the best were still at fifty or sixty and, given their market shares and the ideas they had, it was a bargain. Rogers didn't want to argue with him. She wanted to talk to Kugelman. Kugelman thought about how women were required to wear exercise clothes that revealed their failures whereas men could dress to cover up. That was a conspiracy in itself. Still, he liked her powder blue leotard with the purple stripe despite an instinct to distrust people who ate pineapple muffins. He only ate pineapple if nothing else was left. They got the pineapple for the gentiles, Kugelman quickly determined. Jews don't eat pineapple muffins. Kugelman believed he could identify the landsmen just by their choices in low-fat muffins.

"The pharmaceuticals are underpriced. Lots of failed mergers. They make the products from the biotechs and they will grab the markets," she asserted, eating an entire pumpkin muffin in the time it took her to reveal this. Kugelman didn't seem to care. But then she managed to get his attention by suggesting that the Fed was deliberately stifling the market. Kugelman was suspicious of the Fed also.

Soon there was a club, a kind of postrun muffin club that traded market tips. Five or six regulars sat around the snack bar talking. Kugelman started running a little earlier to assure his acquisition of blueberry muffins, which were the first to go. That was the Jewish influence. The last one to finish running got the bran and the pineapple. Part of the problem was that Jarvis ate too many muffins. You had to get there before him if you didn't want to end up with pineapple.

One thing they all agreed on: in this market, they were all making a lot of money.

"But why aren't we losing any weight?" Kugelman asked.

"If you want to lose weight," offered the small, thin, dark-haired young woman working behind the muffin counter, "acupuncture. I know this acupuncturist, he . . ."

The muffin club stared at her with cold resentment. They were all heavily invested in pharmaceuticals and did not want to hear about "alternative medicine." It suddenly occurred to Kugelman that the woman behind the counter never ate her own muffins. Now why was that?

Jarvis changed the subject because he was excited about Gencorp. A small company, really just a start-up, and a bargain at thirty-seven. But it was going to get a huge market share with something called flomogen2000.

What is it? They all wanted to know. Nobody really knew what it was or what it did but it was said to be the next big thing. But was it smart to buy on the rumor?

Kugelman's idea of a good day was one in which he found the evidence to support one of his theories. Friday, April 23, was a great day for Kugelman. As he chugged into his third mile, with more than four hundred calories burned, he noticed a story from the Bronx about the six-month anniversary of the death of Big Biscuit. His fans reminisced.

"He was, like, a genius, you know."

It was all in the Bronx and the fans all looked and sounded Latino. If he was a Jewish rapper, thought Kugelman, why can't anyone find any Jewish fans to interview? When the reporter said that Big Biscuit's real name was Alonso Rivera, Kugelman was triumphant.

Then Jarvis, while heartlessly consuming the last blueberry muffin and moving to cranberry (as though it were the same thing, Kugelman thought), said something that started putting the evidence together for Kugelman. Flomogen2000, the invention that had made Gencorp's stock rise thirty percent, a leading gainer for the biotech sector, was used in fat-free food!

Kugelman tried to look casual and waited for the muffin club to break up. Rogers waited until the others left. Then she smiled at Kugelman, patiently waiting for his proposition.

Kugelman noticed her look. "Listen," he said, "what do you know about Big Biscuit?"

"Big Biscuit?" she said, at once trying to cover her disappointment but also her panic because she had never heard of Big Biscuit. "It's on the Big Board, right?"

Kugelman patiently waited for Rogers to leave, which she did quickly and nervously, and then, feigning aimlessness, he made his way to the muffin counter, to the thin, dark-haired woman behind the counter who did not eat her own muffins.

"I know what you want," said the woman with a coquettish smile.

"You do?"

The smiling woman insisted that there really were no more blueberry muffins, no more muffins at all until tomorrow.

"You never eat the muffins, do you?"

Turning defensive, she denied ever eating them. Kugelman asked to see a package, a label, anything from the muffin company.

It took three days before Kugelman was able to track down the muffin company, and then a flour company, and eventually establish that the muffins did contain flomogen2000. It was the tobacco debacle all over again. Should he warn Jarvis? It was only a matter of time until it was proven that flomogen2000 was addictive and then some whistle-blower would establish that Gencorp and the muffin company knew it all along. That it had been planned. Then he realized: they had killed Big Biscuit, killed him because he knew, he had found out! Paranoia is a theory without evidence. He sold his Gencorp at seventy—sold on the rumor just like you were supposed to—and made five thousand dollars.

Mrs. Rivera agreed to see him. She lived on a Bronx street off of Prospect Avenue with torn chain-link fences and well-worn brownstone stoops where Jews, including Kugelman's parents, had once sat and gossiped in Yiddish but where today all the gossip was in Spanish.

Kugelman knew that this was the kind of day in which theory after theory would be confirmed.

Except that Mrs. Rivera, in spite of her Spanish accent and her name, seemed Jewish. Kugelman could always tell. She was a small round woman in an apron. She probably always wore the apron in the house so that she would be ready to cook. "Sit down," she said. "It is always good to meet one of Alonso's friends."

Kugelman started to feel guilty. "I'm not really a friend. I never met him."

"Do you want to eat something?"

"Oh, no, thank you."

"Sit down; I'll go get it." All right, thought Kugelman, I could be wrong about her and Alonso not being Jewish.

But then, to Kugelman's horror—it should have been triumph, but it terrified him—Mrs. Rivera came out of the kitchen with a platter stacked two and three high with assorted flavors of muffins.

"They're fat-free," she said. "I still have a freezer full of them. Alonso ate them after his weight started to get out of control." She stared sadly at the muffins. "He liked the pineapple."

Pineapple, Kugelman thought knowingly.

"But they didn't help. I'll show you." She vanished into another room of this dark apartment of overstuffed furniture. He could hear her sifting through things. Somewhere, a radio or television was playing—an all-news station.

She came back with a framed photo of the two of them, mother and son. Big Biscuit was large, but not yet biscuit shaped. What made him look so huge was that his mother, Mrs. Rivera, was not the rounded fleshy elf that he had met, but a tiny wiry woman.

As he looked at the photo he could not help hearing the financial news broadcasting in the other room. The Dow was having a late rally and the NASDAQ was at a record high. "I think they have a chemical in them that makes you keep eating them."

"What chemical—they're good. But they're fattening."

"But they're only sixty calories."

"If you believe that, I'll tell you another one," she said, rolling her eyes. "Here, try this one. It ba-na-na." She winked.

Kugelman could not resist politely reaching for it, though banana was not one of his favorites.

ORANGINA

Vivi and Robo

Most people remember where they lost their virginity but few remember as much about the spot as Robo. He remembered, for example, that it was a twelve percent downhill grade toward the southwest and that the soil under Vivi was ten percent sand with a gravel subsoil and a strong limestone content held together by coarse silt. There was also a touch of calcareous clay, volcanic Lydian stone, and millstone grit.

He also recalled that the soil smelled ripe, slightly moist, surprisingly organic, which was exactly how he remembered Vivi smelling. The leafy plants that had given them privacy in the vineyard were American rootstocks, tough and gnarly little trunks planted by Robo's great-grandfather after his own had been destroyed by blight. Their leaves glowed electric chartreuse from the sunlight above and their grapes were cabernet sauvignon.

They were only fifteen years old that afternoon and had already been in love for more years than anyone could remember. They were simply Vivi and Robo and no one, least of all themselves, ever doubted that they would always be together.

The families were a less than perfect match. Vivi's father was a Socialist; in fact he was the mayor—a feat accomplished through the 878 votes he garnered, seventeen more than his right-wing opponent. Robo's parents never voted for him. They were the owners of a valuable plot of land, one of the few locally owned Bordeaux estates, and were convinced that the political right were the more reliable defenders of property. The left had given up Indochina, Morocco, Tunisia, and even Algeria and he doubted they would ever stand by his land either. But the families got along the way families do in a small town. Even when Vivi's father spoke out against the war in Algeria, they got along. But then, in that troubled year, 1968, something happened that could not be reconciled. It was called Orangina.

Robo was now twenty years old and the farthest he had been from the village of St. Etienne de Gradelle was an afternoon with his father in the city of Bordeaux when he was thirteen years old. For his twentieth birthday his parents gave him a train ticket and money for three days in the capital.

His first day, a warm, sunny day, he was walking up the Boule Miche feeling hot and thirsty, and he noticed a stand that was selling an orange drink in little round bottles the size of oranges. It was cold and, he imagined, refreshing and he ordered one. Robo had a highly trained palate. This drink was very sweet, but it was also bitter with the perfumey taste of orange peel and an intensity that came from effervescence. It seemed perfect for that moment and after he finished it he asked for a second one and was sipping on it when thousands of people his age filled the wide boulevard carrying signs, arms around each other's shoulders— singing "The Internationale."

Suddenly from a side street came a phalanx of uniformed, helmeted police, clubs raised. The demonstrators, who had looked so merry a minute before, were now angrily digging up pavement stones and hurling them at the police. One square stone was heading straight for Robo but he easily sidestepped it by swiveling out into the street, where a policeman planted his black club squarely across the back of his head.

He felt confused, disoriented, as a truck with a whining siren carried him off to jail. The next morning he was released and he went back to the stand on the Boule Miche and had an Orangina, which felt good after a night in jail. Not long after, another demonstration came by and he recognized some of his new friends from jail, who urged him to join them. He did and was arrested again, this time avoiding the crack on the head, which made for a better night in jail. The next morning he was back at the Boule Miche sipping Orangina.

Although a conservative young man from the country, from a rightist family, Robo was angered by the police and their clubs and wanted to see the students overthrow de Gaulle, the mean old general with his troops that hit people while they tried to drink Orangina. Though he could not bring himself to say it out loud, he felt himself becoming a bit "on the left."

When his three days were up and it was time to go home he couldn't because there was a general strike and the trains weren't running. So there were more demonstrations and more Orangina and more visits to jail and even more Orangina. He was beginning to see that de Gaulle was not going to be overthrown and that while change might be a good thing, it was not easy to change anything in France, that France was like the soil in St. Etienne de Gradelle—it never changed and you knew exactly what it could and could not grow.

When the trains were running again Robo bought six round little bottles of Orangina, shoved them in his bag, and returned to St. Etienne de Gradelle. He was not glad to be back. People there did not even know what was going on in Paris. Even Vivi seemed different to him. Vivi was not like the young people he had gone to jail with in Paris. She was like France. She was not going to change.

His parents asked him how he liked Paris and he told them that it was very interesting and that he had learned a great deal. They were pleased because this, after all, was why they had sent him there. People in town would ask him about his trip to Paris and he always said, "It was interesting."

"Eh, oui," they invariably replied in a southern drawl (everything they did they did invariably). "Paris is a real education."

"Eh, oui," Robo would answer.

Margaret and Jarvis

"Café Florent."

"Hello, this is Harold Jarvis. Can you tell me if you have in your cave"—he loved using words like that—"do you by any chance have a Gradelle LeBlanc *soixante-huit*?"

"Nineteen sixty-eight?"

"Yes."

"Bordeaux?"

"Yes."

"I'll check."

This was the night they would make it official. He and Margaret would get married and then they would always remember that they began with Gradelle LeBlanc *soixante-huit*—well, not really began. The beginning was a little tawdry and involved a number of, if he recalled correctly, vodka martinis. All the more reason to have this official beginning with a Gradelle LeBlanc 1968. *The Wine Report* said, "The 1960s are peaking and right now the Gradelle LeBlanc 1968 may be the finest red wine anywhere, not to mention one of the best Grand Crus of all time."

He creased the magazine with the heel of his hand, trying to fix it permanently at this page. The cover had a picture of Margaret's ex-husband and she wouldn't like that.

"It's not on the list but I can have the wine steward check in the cellar. Some of the old specialties are not listed."

In the meantime Jarvis called a few other restaurants known for their caves, with no luck. Then Café Florent called back.

"We have it!"

"Fantastic, how many bottles do you have?"

"You know, sir, it is three hundred fifteen dollars a bottle."

"But you have more than one? Can I reserve one?"

"We have two. But you can reserve one if you like."

"Well, it was the pick of the month in *The Wine Report*."

"Well, you will have one waiting for you tonight."

Vivi and Robo

"Try this," Robo said, the bottle making a slight hissing noise. Vivi sipped the Orangina and smiled, a conspiratorial smile, a comradely smile, a smile, it seemed to Robo, not unlike the ones the demonstrators gave him when he had joined them. Robo felt a little better. At least here was something from his trip to Paris he could share with Vivi. He had told her about the demonstrations and going to jail and she had looked troubled—not disapproving but worried. But the Orangina she really liked. "Can we let Denise try?"

Denise, Vivi's close friend, loved Orangina. Her father owned the café. She got him to order a case and soon many cases. In the late afternoon all of the young people of town would sit at tables sipping Orangina while the workers stood in blue overalls at the bar angrily sipping red wine.

Vivi's father, the Socialist mayor, was at first pleased by this development. He too enjoyed a midafternoon Orangina. He felt that it was an exciting new part of the new spirit of the time, what was becoming known as "the spirit of '68." In Czechoslovakia there was Dubcek and the Prague Spring; Danny the Red was in Paris; Rudi the Red was in Germany. And in St. Etienne de Gradelle there was Orangina.

But the mayor didn't understand that bold acts have their consequences. The union leaders complained. The wine growers association complained. "This is Bordeaux," said the deputy mayor, who had drunk so much Bordeaux in his life that he had a Bordeaux-colored nose. "The people of this town cannot be sitting around sipping Orangina instead of wine. This is a *vin rouge* town."

But the issue became more complicated. It became tied to the Algerian war. Orangina had been made in Algeria until 1962 when the French withdrew and took Orangina with them. So those who had supported the war, including Robo's father, supported Orangina. Robo's father would wait until the union leaders went to the café for their late afternoon *quart rouge* and he would walk in and with great fanfare, right in front of the leaders, he would pour the bright fizzy elixir down his throat while staring at them. In the same way he used to gulp mouthfuls of his own unlicensed brandy in front of magistrates.

"Marcel," the red-nosed deputy pleaded with the mayor, "you have to do something. If we lose the union support, we are out in the next election."

"What can I do"—the mayor shrugged—"ban Orangina?"

"Exactly!"

"I was joking," the mayor said defensively. But the wine growers association wanted the ban and the unions wanted the ban and the mayor had to get 865 votes from somewhere and so he decreed a ban on the selling of Orangina in St. Etienne de Gradelle.

The LeBlancs still had Orangina because Robo's father

drove into Bordeaux and bought it by the case. It was a defiant political act and he would deliberately take swigs from the little bottles in public places. In reality, anyone could have gotten the drink the same way he did, but it never occurred to most people in St. Etienne de Gradelle to ever leave town.

Robo didn't like his father's politics but he did like his Orangina and he would grab two bottles and hide them in a bag and meet Vivi and they would go to their spot in the vineyard and sit on the moist ground and drink Orangina where no one would see them. They could only imagine the scandal if the mayor's daughter was caught drinking Orangina in the vineyard. But that was part of the fun too. Robo stroked the damp soil and rubbed it between his finger and thumb and said, "You know, I think we're going to have a great wine this year." Then he lifted his little round bottle and sucked in the last mouthful of Orangina.

Margaret and Jarvis

It was breathing all through the appetizer. Decanted in crystal, the roast venison arriving, the time had now come for Jarvis and for the Gradelle LeBlanc *soixante-huit*. It was to be poured in glasses as big as fishbowls. Margaret patted her lips with her napkin in anticipation. The wine was black. Even with the glass tilted, it was black to its very edge, like a thick syrup. It smelled of so many things, different fruits and woods, that it seemed almost unnecessary to drink it. Whole five-course meals did not have as many flavors as a tiny sip of this wine, and a single sip kept tasting for minutes.

"It's the cigar box," Jarvis finally said. "Just that little hint of cigar box that ties the rest of it together."

Margaret smiled, a bit condescendingly, and thought, I don't taste any cigar box.

He seemed to read her mind. "That's the beauty. It's very subtle. Not like those California cabs that taste like they were poured from a cigar box."

Margaret just shook her head in the negative. Cabs, she thought. Why do Americans have to talk like that? Margaret was Canadian.

Jarvis reached into his pocket and pulled out his carefully folded magazine. "I'll read from *The Wine Report*."

They always want to say things like "cabs" or "pinots" to show that they are on a first-name basis with the grapes, Margaret thought. She was in an irritable mood. But it was true. Americans want to be on a first-name basis with everything. They never talk about where wines are from. Only the type of grape. That's because all of their wines are bad imitations of wine from somewhere else. They used to be more honest. If they made a bad imitation of a red burgundy, they called it "red burgundy." Now they call it "pinot noir." Taste my pinot, she thought. Then she saw the cover of Jarvis's magazine. "Can I see that?"

Too late. Margaret reached over and took it, unfolding it so that the cover showed. "Goddamn it, that pisses me off."

"Oh, that. Forget about it," Jarvis said, trying to sound casual. The cover showed his picture with the caption "Robert Eggle Takes On Rieslings."

"What the hell does he know about Rieslings!" She was almost shouting.

"Shh!"

Her voice dropped to a strained hoarse whisper. "He wouldn't know a Riesling from a ginger ale. How does he get away with this? The expert." She stabbed her venison with a fork as though to stop it from leaping. "He wouldn't know it from his goddamn pinot," she said, taking an angry mouthful and washing it down with the old black Bordeaux.

"This is what he knows. Our tenth anniversary I gave him a bag of Hawaiian sea salt. You know, the red one."

"Nice," Jarvis said, not quite as authentically as he would have liked to have sounded.

"I mean, it's rare stuff, right? I had to special order it from a catalog too. You couldn't just order online then. It comes from Hawaii! Wonderful on fish. And full of symbolism. Polynesian. It means lasting forever. Well, I knew right then it wasn't lasting at all. I could see he had no idea what it was. He just stared at it stupidly. He probably didn't even know it was our anniversary. He has a terrible memory. Now he's giving advice?" She took another angry gulp of wine.

Vivi and Robo

Politics were running amok as they often do in the *sud-ouest*. The mayor could now see that the ban was not going to get him his 865 votes. Served him right, he thought, to listen to that drunk of a deputy. The right wing was against him for banning the Orangina, but they never voted Socialist anyway. But a lot of young people were angry about the ban too. The young people were leftist and mobilized. If they voted with the right, or just refused to vote, which a lot were saying they would, the next mayor of St. Etienne de Gradelle would be a conservative. And the first thing he would do would be to bring back Orangina.

But the situation quickly became more difficult for everyone. Pampi Gallard decided that he wanted to be mayor. Pampi was that rare man who had little to gain or lose from politics. His father was the doctor and he was only a year away from being a doctor too. In the meantime, he thought it would be fun to be mayor and maybe he could impress someone like Vivi if he were mayor. Of course, he could only be mayor by unseating her father. Still, he reasoned, she would be impressed with someone who was mayor like her father. And if it did not work out, he would still be the doctor. He formed his own political party, the Naranjists. Orangina, it seems, was invented by a Spaniard who called it Naranjina.

The principal platform of the Parti Naranjist was to legalize Orangina in St. Etienne, and there were always good turnouts for party rallies because they gave away free Orangina. The movement spread throughout the *sud-ouest*, though beyond St. Etienne it took on other ideas. In the summer of 1968, as de Gaulle reestablished his authority, throughout the *sud-ouest* the Parti Naranjist became a party for reactionaries who believed de Gaulle was not dealing harshly enough with the rebellious left. But in St. Etienne de Gradelle it remained a party for people who liked Orangina.

The Naranjist slogan was "France will always remain France." The first time Robo heard the slogan he snickered, "That's exactly what's wrong with France."

The leading pollsters showed the Naranjists taking St. Etienne but also doing well in a few major centers including possibly even Bordeaux.

But in St. Etienne there was only one poll that mattered, only one that anyone believed. Patrice de Gironde, who owned the *épicerie*, periodically asked the first ten rightists and the first ten leftists to come into the store—everyone knew everyone's politics—who they were supporting and from this sampling determined election results with unerring accuracy. And he discovered something different from the standard pollsters. He found that the Naranjists were drawing off the right vote far more than the Socialist vote. There would be a three-way split with the Socialists having the most votes, the right the least, and no one with a majority. In the runoff, however, according to de Gironde, the Naranjists could edge out the Socialists because of the young Socialists who were angry about the Orangina ban. Of course, de Gironde was not completely neutral, because he wanted to sell Orangina in his store, so he took his polling data to the Hôtel de Ville to show the mayor. He tried to convince him that by dropping the Orangina ban, he would catch the right unprepared and he could win as many as nine hundred votes. The mayor looked out his window and in the town square he could see Pampi greeting a huge crowd, everyone with an Orangina in hand. He wore a bright orange paper hat, the symbol of the party.

"The next mayor, monsieur?" said Patrice.

The mayor looked at Pampi and he knew what he had to do.

Margaret and Jarvis

"That's why we broke up," Margaret growled and then drank more wine. "He lost all interest in what I ate. He acted like I was committing some kind of social injustice by appreciating good things."

"Margaret," Jarvis said patiently while swirling his wine in its fishbowl glass, "let's not spend all night talking about Robert."

"Expert. Now he's the expert."

"Margaret, please."

She took a deep sip. "And there is no way there is any fucking cigar box to this wine."

"There is. It's subtle, balanced with the strawberry, but it's there. It's a thing with cabs."

"Well, maybe we should ask Robert fucking Eggle when he gets through with his goddamn Rieslings."

"Margaret . . ."

She reached over to dust a speck off his shoulder but it was more like a swat.

Vivi and Robo

Claude stared at the sky with his pale blue eyes set deep in his craggy face, the kind of face that looked like it had spent all its time staring at the sky. "I say we don't take the risk. We harvest now and we have one of our best years. It's been a perfect year up until now."

"In one more week it will be the best year," Robo insisted.

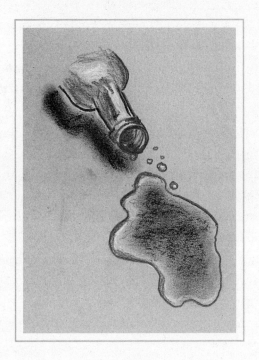

"Unless it rains, then it will be nothing."

Robo slapped Claude on the back. "It'll hold. Have some faith. A few clouds. It won't rain. This is the *sud-ouest*."

Claude stared at Robo dubiously.

"One of the great Bordeaux of history, isn't it worth the wait? Greatness takes guts."

Claude smiled and Robo smiled back and they shook hands and walked through the vineyard together. When he saw Vivi later that day he finally told her that he was only staying until the '68 was barreled.

"Then where are you going?" said Vivi, trembling.

"I'm going to America. To California."

They stared at each other. As far back as either of them could remember this was the first time they realized that they were not going to spend their lives together.

"Come with me," he said. "We'll start a winery. What Americans won't do to have a real French winemaker."

But he knew that Vivi was never leaving St. Etienne.

"No Orangina in America," she said with a weak smile.

"Maybe I'll import it. It's America. Anything is possible."

Margaret and Jarvis

Peter, the waiter, came to Margaret and Jarvis's abandoned table to retrieve the handsome tip left in a stack of twenty-dollar bills. Then he noticed, incredulously, that about two glasses of wine still remained in the carafe. After studying the label on the bottle and confirming, yes, it was the Gradelle LeBlanc 1968, his first instinct was to hide it. He took the long cork, lying ceremoniously on its silver coaster, and examined it. Then he wrapped the bottle, the carafe, and the cork in napkins and took them to the kitchen, laying them carefully in a forgotten corner behind some aprons.

Peter went back to work but during the evening he remembered that his wife was not drinking because she was pregnant. He called her up and tried to convince her that one taste would not hurt. "It's a three-hundred-dollar Bordeaux. You may never get another chance."

She was unmoved. And so Peter decided to share it with two other waiters when the restaurant closed. They poured it into the big fishbowl glasses and clinked them together, still standing up in the kitchen, and they tasted in silence. The tastes swirled in their mouths. "So this is what three-hundred-dollar wine tastes like," Peter said.

"It doesn't taste like fifty-dollar wine," another said, and the three laughed in agreement.

"Can you imagine," the third waiter said, "being so rich you could leave this behind?"

"This is about eighty dollars' worth."

"Do you realize," said Peter, "about sixty dollars of the tip was from this bottle alone?"

"Did they leave a good one?"

"Oh, yes."

Then Arnaud came through the door and the waiters stiffened. But he walked past the ones sipping Gradelle '68 and went up to the porter sipping on a small bottle of Orangina. "Take it easy with that stuff," said Arnaud. "It's expensive."

Vivi

It didn't rain and Robo stayed just long enough for everyone to realize that his was going to be a great wine. Even the Paris writers said so. So did someone from London. But she couldn't leave with him. Her father lifted the ban on Orangina and was reelected. Three years later she married Pampi, who had become a doctor like he was supposed to and had given up politics. Once he abandoned politics Vivi's father managed to like him, somewhat. Villages have a way of working out these differences. Vivi lived a happy life in St. Etienne de Gradelle, the kind of life she had always imagined for herself.

The day before her wedding, Vivi had wandered into the vineyard. She went to the spot and looked at the sandy soil and at the new vines starting to sprout chartreuse shoots, translucent in the sunlight. She wondered how it could be that you could have an unfulfilled destiny, that something could be destined to be and yet somehow not happen.

BEAN CURD

Minty Maris adjusted the white taped bandage on her forehead and checked the bunny in her purse, a slightly threadbare tan bunny whose ears no longer stood up like they used to but which seemed perfectly comfortable in her canvas bag. Minty shuddered when she thought of that black Italian bag she had just replaced. That soft leather—soft as a bunny.

Out of the sunlight Minty and the bunny walked into Luigi's. A walnut-skinned Indian man in a white shirt and black vest saw her come in and walked across the dark empty room with a smile so big, so sudden, his face could barely hold it.

"Hello, Luigi," she said warmly, fully aware that the

chances were his name was not Luigi. But Luigi was the only name she had and he had accepted it so graciously for the past eight months that she was beginning to think maybe that really was his name. Somebody had that name back when Luigi's had been an Italian restaurant. She had loved the Italian Luigi's and had been disappointed when the food had changed. But they never changed the name. Now it was vegan but Minty kept coming because it was the restaurant she went to. By chance, after several months of dining in this vegan restaurant, she too became vegan. She had made this conversion so recently that she had only just found out that the word was pronounced with a hard "g."

"I am a vedjan," she would say and no one contradicted her until her older daughter did recently with an irritated tone.

Luigi, whatever his name might be, tried to treat her well. She always called in advance to reserve a booth and he always held one for her.

"I called and reserved a booth," she reminded him.

"Yes, mum, we have it for you," he assured with a polite little bow and a sweep of his arm to usher her into the next dark empty room.

And there it was. A booth saved for Mrs. Maris. Luigi led the way and Minty followed with her bunny and her bandaged forehead, past the banks of empty red leather booths to the one with the black sign with white block letters: RESERVED.

Minty happily slid into the booth, thinking to herself,

Luigi always saves a booth for me, as though the empty room was too dark for her to realize that she was alone. It used to be full, but Minty was ashamed of those days when she used to eat the flesh of abused baby animals and pasta made from the eggs of unborn chickens.

Luigi took her cloth coat to hang it up. Her bag fell to the side and the bunny fell on the floor. He adroitly picked it up and started to give it a comfortable place on the booth. "That's all right, Luigi," said Mrs. Maris impatiently, holding out her arm to take back the stuffed animal. He thinks I'm crazy, she thought to herself. Some strange lady that takes stuffed animals to lunch.

People never really understood why she and her husband liked stuffed animals. They weren't their friends. They were just stuffed animals. But their daughters had always had them and for a dozen years they had been part of the family life and they got used to them, how soft and sweet faced and big eyed they were, the sensation of hugging one at night. And they all carried memories. Her younger daughter was given this one in a package in the mail from a cousin on her fourth birthday. She named it Sweet Postie and hugged it for the next three days. Now her daughters complained about their mother bringing Postie everywhere, but Minty argued, "Just a nice custom."

Minty's husband explained it differently. He said, "'My life has crept so long on a broken wing / Thro' cells of madness, haunts of horror and fear, / That I come to be grateful at last for a little thing.' "

This didn't help at all. It clarified nothing and, in truth, badly overdramatized, overstated the whole thing. But it was Tennyson and he loved Tennyson. When he retired, getting out of the aluminum boom at just the right moment, with what was said to be a fortune, and he still in his forties, everyone asked, "What will you do?" and he answered, "Read poetry." And that was largely what he had been doing, mostly the Victorians, that and bird hunting. The hunting was over now, of course.

Minty patted the bandage on her forehead. "Did I tell you how I got this?"

"No, mum," said Luigi. "How is your bump?" Making clear that, in fact, he had heard the story. She knew that he had. But a good story always bears repeating.

"You hear these stories about how someone's life is forever changed by a blow to the head, but you don't imagine it really happening."

"No, mum."

"We were turkey shooting. God forgive me, just out there looking for the poor things to kill. Thomas is retired, you know."

"Your husband, mum?"

"No, no. Well, yes, he is retired too. But he is Matthew. Thomas is a dog. A German shorthaired pointer. He was the first to see. He wouldn't hunt anymore. It probably wouldn't have happened if he were there. But he just wouldn't hunt anymore. Refused. So we were in the brush and Matthew was reciting something. What was it? He was supposed to be doing turkey calls, but he was reciting from the Brownings or something. No, Yeats—'Where flapping herons wake / The drowsy water rats.' Something that rhymes with 'faery vats.' He knows these things. Yeats. Definitely."

"Yes, mum," said Luigi, pointedly placing the menu in front of her, eager to return to the silent corner where he normally stood.

"Suddenly," she resolutely continued, "I saw an eye. An angry red eye. It was a turkey eye and it seemed to be saying, 'How dare you!' and then in his rage, he flew up from the brush—turkeys don't fly much—he flew up with that flaming eye and smacked me in the head. So hard it knocked me down and I was practically unconscious. And when I woke up I realized that I could never again be responsible for the killing of another living thing."

"So are you ready to order, mum?"

Minty suddenly realized the menu was in her hands and said, "The bean curd special, please."

"I'm just telling you don't do it," said Grace, rocking her baby against her shoulder.

"Oh, God," said Emma, slumping in a chair. "It's—it's Camp Winnisacko all over again."

"Camp Winni...? Listen, Mom's on this vegetarian thing. So I think we should just do Thanksgiving ourselves. And you want to do this over the turkey? There won't even be a turkey. Mom thinks she's some kind of turkey advocate!"

"I remember when you did it."

"Yes," said Grace, abruptly changing her tone and smiling dreamily at her baby. "It was how Dad proposed to Mom, you know. That's how we got the idea." It was family legend and mostly true. Thanksgiving at Bunko and Mugs's. No one remembered why Minty's parents were called Bunko and Mugs. Probably in the same no-longer-remembered process in which their daughter Marianne became Minty. According to the story, Bunko brought out the turkey and set it on the table and was about to start carving. Everyone was applauding the turkey and suddenly Matthew, who was still speaking prose in those days, shouted above the noise to Minty, "Will you marry me!" Minty was said to shout back, "Yes!" and then everyone was applauding them and Bunko tore into the turkey with a knife, hacking it up because he never learned how to carve a bird.

"You and Morris did the same thing," Emma asserted.

"Well, he had already proposed. I guess he was afraid I would turn him down." Grace giggled. "But I had told him about Mom and Dad and he thought it was very romantic."

"Mom," said Grace's other daughter, Maya, impatiently.

"What, Maya?" said Grace.

"Can I have some candy?"

"We don't have any more."

"It was romantic," Emma insisted. "I remember. All those nice bone-colored linens and that fine porcelain with the little gilded edges and a really black old Bordeaux in those cut Waterford goblets."

"I can't believe you remember the wine."

"What about the Halloween candy?" said Maya with the rugged persistence of a five-year-old.

"Gone," said Grace. "You ate it all."

Maya stared at her mother. They both knew she was lying.

"It was Gradelle LeBlanc. And calla lilies. Yellow and white calla lilies in that long crystal vase. And Dad came out with the biggest turkey I think I have ever seen."

"Twenty-eight pounds. I remember it was a twenty-eight-pounder. Dad could barely hold the platter. He carried it from the kitchen running like he had to pee."

"All right," said Maya. "A cookie." Her fallback position.

"Just one," said Grace, not even realizing what her daughter knew, that she had lost the round.

"It was roasted perfectly," Emma insisted. "And the skin just crackled and steam filled the dining room with the most unbelievable smell. Everyone applauded. Dad picked up the knife with the ivory handle."

"Bone. Mom probably won't use it anymore."

"And Morris shouted, 'We are going to get married!' and everybody turned to you and kept applauding. And Dad . . ."

"Dad, like some kind of Viking, ripped a drumstick off the poor bird and waved it in the air."

"It was the most wonderful moment."

"Even then he was a cornball. But at least he talked about business and real things. Listen to me. This year, there won't be any turkey and Dad is just going to babble Tennyson or something. It just won't work."

"You see, it's Camp Winnisacko again."

"Camp Winnisacko?"

"See, you don't even remember."

"I remember going there."

"Right, you went there every summer, and every summer I heard about how wonderful it was, how perfect it was. I dreamed of being big enough for Camp Winnisacko and then when my time came . . ." Emma clapped her hands loudly, smacking them with such force that they stung. "Suddenly wonderful Camp Winnisacko isn't any good anymore and I can't go."

"The head counselor was caught molesting children."

"Yes. That's what everyone said as soon as it was *my* chance."

"And another one turned out to be a big drug dealer."

"So you even got to have good drugs. But no wonderful Camp Winnisacko for Emma."

"I'll talk to Mom about Thanksgiving. I don't know how

this will work, but I'll talk to her. Does Larry know he is going to have in-laws who play with stuffed animals?"

"Hello," Matthew said cheerfully into the phone while stroking the soft nylon fur of his stuffed St. Bernard, Rico.

"Hi, Dad. It's Grace."

"Ah, 'This is my son, mine own Telemachus, / To whom I leave the scepter and the isle—'"

"Dad, would you just put Mom on?" said Grace.

There was a long silence until Minty came to the telephone.

"Mom, Emma really wants you to do Thanksgiving. She wants to bring Larry."

"Well, of course she can."

"So you are going to do Thanksgiving?"

"Yes, of course."

"I thought that maybe with your new diet, and your feeling about turkeys—"

"If you had seen the look in that bird's eye, Grace. A look of complete—of indignation. Indignation and righteous anger. This little red dot of fury that—"

"So you're not going to do Thanksgiving."

"I am. I am. You think it takes one little bump on the head to stop me? I'll be fine."

"But what kind of meal are you going to make?"

"The usual. But it will just be vedjan."

"Vegan. But there needs to be a turkey."

"There will be a turkey. I promise."

"One you can take out and carve."

"One you can take out and carve. A big vedjan turkey. Trust me, it will be wonderful. And it won't cost the life of one living thing."

"I'll bring a pumpkin pie—a big, old-fashioned, traditional pumpkin pie. Okay?"

"Just as long as it's vedjan, dear. Don't forget, no egg—including the crust, dear."

"Okay, I'll bring cranberry sauce."

"Just as long as it's vedjan."

"Vegan."

There was a pause. "And you begone. Farewell, dear."

"No, God, you are talking to Dad too much. I was just saying, the word is 'vegan.'"

"Well," Minty said uncertainly. "And the word was good. Adieu." And she hung up the telephone.

It arrived four days before Thanksgiving, which was when the turkey used to be delivered. "It's heavy," said Matthew, carrying the carton to the kitchen.

"Twenty pounds," said Minty excitedly.

Carefully, with a formality close to ritual, Matthew opened the box, pulled out the large squishy object in white plastic, and tested it surreptitiously with a squeeze from the fingertips, as though it were a woman's breast and no one was looking. Minty saw it and smiled—smiled to say, I bet it feels wonderful, doesn't it? She reached over and squeezed it, permission for him to squeeze it again too. Twenty pounds of bean curd has a wonderful buoyant feel.

The white plastic bag said:

TOFURKEY—VEGAN TURKEY

100 percent organically produced soy bean curd

Baste and roast exactly like a turkey

Matthew placed it on a platter in its plastic bag in the refrigerator.

They looked at it through the open door, the refrigerator light giving macabre highlights to their faces.

"Do you think it will be good?" asked Minty timidly, stroking Totty, the green fluffy turtle that Grace had once won at a fair.

Matthew shrugged.

"At least nothing will have died for it," she said.

He closed the refrigerator door and recited, " 'Long have I sigh'd for a calm: God grant I may find it at last!' "

" 'Maud,' " Minty whispered shyly. "It's Tennyson's 'Maud.' "

Matthew smiled happily and absentmindedly stroked Rico, the stuffed St. Bernard.

. . .

Over the next few days leading up to the holiday, questions arose from time to time.

"It says to cook like a turkey. But a twenty-pound turkey could cook five hours. Do you think they mean that?"

"That's what it says," was Matthew's confident ruling. But later he started musing on the large curd. "Do you think there will be leftovers? I always liked the leftovers. All those sandwiches."

Minty patted the bandage on her forehead. She did that when she suspected her husband of wavering.

In bed, just before falling asleep on the eve of the holiday, Minty whispered, "Do you think it's supposed to be trussed up with string like a turkey?"

"No," said Matthew. "Let it be free."

Minty smiled. "Free-range bean curd."

"Tofurkey."

"Wild tofurkey," she answered.

"'Loud howls the wind, sharp patters the rain, / And the knight sinks back on his pillows again,'" he muttered as he sank his head into his pillow and shut his eyes.

"Matthew?" Minty asked.

But her husband just smiled and said, "Yes, Matthew. Matthew Arnold," and fell asleep clutching Rico.

They got up early on Thanksgiving morning. Minty prepared the baste. Cold-pressed extra virgin olive oil, slices of garlic cloves, a squirt from a lemon, a splash of soy sauce, two twists of black pepper from the pepper mill, fresh rosemary—rosemary was an evergreen and all that was left from her herb garden. She brushed this gently on the vegan turkey. She baked it in a medium oven and every half hour she took it out and basted it so that by the time the guests arrived the entire house was infused with a Mediterranean perfume.

As each guest entered, full of doubts and trepidations, the scent from the roasting bean curd reassured them, made them feel that it would all be well after all, that it was just Thanksgiving and the rumors of Minty's new and peculiar food ways were grossly exaggerated. She always did know how to cook.

Everyone was reassured, that is, except Maya, who inquired about dessert and could not conceal her anxiety when Grandma Minty said something about soya cake. Larry was visibly nervous, moving his fingers on the lapel of his wool jacket as though he were picking off the herringbones one by one. When he greeted Matthew, Matthew took his hand warmly and said, "'I know him by his harp of gold, / Famous in Arthur's court of old; / I know him by his forest-dress—'"

They were still shaking hands and Larry was trying to smile when Emma muttered through clenched teeth, "What's with the stuffed dog, Dad?"

"Don't start. Just don't start," counseled Grace in a low voice.

"Rico," said Matthew, looking at the stuffed St. Bernard. "You used to love Rico. Never had a meal without him. . . ."

"Tindy."

"What?"

"His name was Tindy. Rico was a pink angora cat."

"Oh, that's right!" Matthew exclaimed and exited the room. He returned triumphantly, petting a pink ball of nylon fur. "It's Rico!"

"Yes," said Emma in a flat voice.

Still, when Emma smelled the basted roast, when she saw the fine cream-colored linens, the black Bordeaux in the cut crystal, the vase with pinkish lilies and bluish hydrangeas, she couldn't help but feel that it was going to be fine, and that she would have her moment. She even thought the bean curd might work out, though when she said something about it her father corrected her.

"Tofurkey."

"What?"

"It's called tofurkey. That's what it said on the plastic it was sealed in."

"Isn't it interesting," said Emma, "that when you buy health food it comes completely sealed so that you know no one has been tampering with it? If you bought a turkey you might not know who was touching it."

"Who would be touching it?" Matthew asked but Emma shrugged off the question and Matthew offered a line from Edward Thomas, the lesser-known Welshman: " 'Like the touch of rain she was. . . .' "

Emma strained to find relevance in this. She could never decide if her father was irritating because a conversation with him always lost direction or admirable because he never had an agenda.

Soon they were all seated with large napkins at their places, thighs draped with linen, sipping Bordeaux, and Matthew came in from the kitchen carrying the large fine porcelain platter with gilded edges and on it, the golden brown roast, hazy with herbal steam.

Everyone applauded.

"You did make a turkey!" Larry declared.

"Oh, no," Minty answered, patting the bandage on her forehead. "And you wouldn't either if you had seen what I saw."

Grace's baby let out a long sliding wail.

Matthew picked up the carving tools, still the ones with the bone handles—apparently they had missed that detail—but then he became lost in "Dover Beach."

"'Sophocles long ago / Heard it on the Ægæan, and it brought / Into his mind the turbid ebb and flow / Of human misery . . .'"

"Dad, for God's sake, what are you talking about?"

The baby unleashed a wail like the blast of a fire truck.

"Grace," Morris shouted, "he's laughing. The baby is laughing!"

"Is there going to be ice cream with the cake?" Maya wanted to know.

"I tell you I could see the hatred in the red little eye—"

"'. . . we / Find also in the sound a thought. . . .'"

"Where is the camera, Grace? It's his first laugh!"

They were all shouting so loudly. Emma realized the moment was about to be stolen by the baby's first laugh and in her panic she barked to Larry, "Tell them! Tell them now!" Finally she screamed it. *"Tell them!"*

And they all stopped talking and looked at Emma.

Larry, as though in an attempt to get their attention, said almost apologetically, "We're getting married."

The family stared for another second in silence and then a sound like the bubbling of thick oatmeal was heard and everyone looked at the platter with the gilded edges just in time to see the lovely brushed surface of the golden brown basted twenty-pound bean curd crack and fall away, revealing a crumble of white geometric fragments spreading in a springy cubist heap over the platter—the collapse of a tofurkey.

The baby wailed again and this time it seemed certain that it was not laughter. Emma and Larry's moment had passed. Only Tindy, the stuffed St. Bernard who had no choice, was smiling.

THE ICING ON THE CAKE

There were problems from the very beginning. First of all it wasn't her birthday. It was Julia's. Julia's mom had brought the cupcakes to school. When they were brought out Maya knew exactly which one was hers. And that was another problem. There was only one cupcake with that high swirl of white icing and sprinkles of every color like a rainbow.

Julia, the birthday girl, got to pick first, and yup, didn't it figure, she picked Maya's. Well, Maya would deal with this in a minute.

The fact was that when the cupcakes were brought out Maya was still working on her drawing of ducks landing at an airport. She had just a little more orange to do. But maybe also a touch of purple. And some green . . .

Now she was satisfied with her drawing and she surveyed the situation. There were only two left—a sickly-looking lemon and a chocolate. This was good. She ran to the tray and grabbed the chocolate. Not that she liked chocolate, but she understood its negotiating power. The girl who had chocolate could always cut a deal. Life was full of possibilities for someone who had chocolate.

Then Maya remembered, Julia was allergic to chocolate. She surveyed the room. This was going to be more complicated than she had thought. But there was Charles, big chubby Charles in his big blue sweater with his hair sticking up.

"Charles," Maya whispered. "Charles."

Charles turned warily.

"Charles, your cupcake has pink icing."

Charles lowered his stare to his cupcake.

"Pink is for girls."

Panic began to reshape his rounded face but fortunately she was there to help him. She handed him the paper plate with the chocolate cupcake and grabbed his pink one and headed straight for Zoe, shy little Zoe, who she noticed had a cupcake with a rose made of yellow icing.

And finally, to Julia, the birthday girl with the mound of white icing and a rainbow of sprinkles. "Julia, I saved this for you. A rose for the birthday girl." And Maya gave her a little kiss as she exchanged cupcakes.

And then it was hers.

She carefully wrapped it and placed it in her lunch box just in time. Her mother was here for her. Walking her home, Grace, her mother, suggested stopping for "a bite to eat."

"No, thank you."

"Just a little something before music class."

"Music class," Maya repeated with a voice of despair.

"Yes, it's Wednesday."

Maya was silent and then, unable to come up with a more elaborate tactic, she said, "I don't want to go to music class today."

"You always like it."

"My stomach hurts."

"Really? Since when?"

"School. Julia had a birthday party and I ate too many candies and cookies."

"Well, see, that's what happens. And we are supposed to go see Grandma Minty later."

"I don't like toe goo!"

"Tofu, dear. Maybe she'll have vegetables."

"My stomach hurts."

Grace took Maya home.

"I think I am going to go lie down in my room for a while."

But Grace stopped her. "Let me take your lunch box."

This froze her for a moment. "Couldn't I play with it in my room? There is nothing in it. I ate all my lunch."

At last. Maya was alone in her room with the lunch box. She had made it. She looked around the room and chose her favorite place, under the bed. There she stretched out in the safety of darkness and opened the lunch box.

There it was, white icing piled high and a rainbow of sprinkles. Even in the under-the-bed darkness she could make out the bright colors. Carefully with her tongue she swept the uppermost peak. Then a little more. The sweetness tickled the roof of her mouth as the icing filled her mouth, thick and rich, and then slowly melted away, trickling down her throat. The sprinkles were little crunches. She licked more. A nice-sized glob fell to the floor. She licked the floor. Some got on her fingers and she licked them. She filled her mouth again and again until she had carefully licked the top of the cupcake clean, leaving only a yellowish mound of cake behind.

Then she took the crumbling mound to the kitchen. "Here, Mom. They gave us muffins in school."

"What's that on your face?"

Maya stuck her tongue as far out as it would go and licked around her mouth. One last taste. Next week was William's birthday and Maya wondered what his mother was going to bring.

THE SOUP

Mrs. Janie Powell Joseph peered deep into the steamy stockpot with approval and put the lid back on slightly ajar, to let just a little steam escape—warm, fish-laden puffs to fill her trailer. The dish was known in her language as "the Soup." In her language she was called "Light before Dawn." But no one called her that anymore because no one spoke her language.

She looked out the small window of her aluminum trailer to the flat land—miles of it, with summer grasses, the truest green she knew, and summer flowers giving little flecks of color. She could see past the one-story houses of Anchorage to the berry-stain purple mountains. And that was as far as she could see. One day the roofs would go all the way to the mountains. She felt a shudder run through her and she went back to the stove to stir the Soup again, as though she needed the steam for its heat.

Then back to the window, to the berry-stained mountains, the purple wall on her horizon, beyond which she could not see. She knew what was there. The black sea and the blue lake, Lake Kish'da y'k, the Lake of the People, and above it, rising like a god's frightening love, the white-crowned dark face of Mount Kish'da y'k, the Mountain of the People, her faraway home, just a few enormous crests of Alaska away.

Back to the Soup, the flavor of the steam feeding her through the pores of her skin. It always made her remember Salmon Lady, who fed her the Soup, and later taught her to make it, and how she made it for Rocky Coast and how he loved it and how she loved him. All gone; now there was only she, Janie Powell Joseph, in Anchorage and there was still the Soup.

The telephone rang. She knew no one anymore. They were all gone. They didn't use telephones anyway. But it had come with the trailer she bought when her land was sold. And she liked the telephone, the possibility that someone would call.

"Heller? Mrs. Janie Powell Joseph. Are how you afternoon?"

It was that professor. They had a bargain. She was the last to speak her language. The last native speaker of the

Kish'da y'k people left behind on earth. For what purpose she had been left behind, she did not yet know.

He wanted to learn her language and speaking to her was his only way to learn. She spoke with him to speak with someone. To speak again in the Language. So she told him that she was home making fish soup and if he wanted to, he could come over.

"Thank it so much, Mrs. Joseph. I be there in a right off." The professor did not yet speak the Language very well.

"Yes, yes, yes," she said, hanging up the phone and stirring the Soup. Soon she heard a hollow tapping on the aluminum door and an intruding voice that slapped the air, flat as the smack of a beaver tail. "Mrs. Powell! Are it I, Dr. Krauss."

She gave a last stir to the Soup and closed the lid on the pot, like tucking a child in safely for bed, before opening the door. "Hello, leader Krauss," she greeted him in the Language, which had no word for doctor. "So good of you to come by."

"Oh, not necessarily. Happily to see one, and spoke the Language of the People."

"Yes," she said, "it feels very good to speak the Language."

"Mmm," he said. "Smells it so good here. What cook you?"

"Oh, it's just something the People make." She looked a little embarrassed. "It's a fish soup. The People always make it. Especially in the late summer when the salmon spawn and float." She stopped a brief second to appreciate nature's idea of spawning and then dying. Wouldn't it be better to die when your purpose had been served?

"The white people don't like the spawned salmon. But the bears eat them and the People make this soup."

"What called it?" Dr. Krauss asked, his pen cocked and notebook flipped open.

"We call it the Soup. . . . Or we did. It's a fish soup."

Dr. Krauss wrote down the name and studied it on the page and then said in English, "Why, that means 'the soup.'"

"Yes," she continued in the Language, "the Soup. It's a fish soup. Salmon. I would invite you to stay but white people never like it."

"Then you no one have share with it?" he said, returning to the Language.

"Not many," she said with a sad smile. "There are a few of the People left. Half-and-half people, like the old story of the woman who married the dog."

It was a story that many Alaskan people told and Krauss just nodded. He knew the story. "And the half people speak not the Language."

She smiled because she was too polite to laugh. "You speak the Language better than half people. They go to white school and forget everything."

"And your son?"

"He is not a half people," she said defensively.

"No," he quickly agreed. "I can suppose that. Some doubt the last of the People he, I to guess."

"Yes," she said. "I suppose he is the last. But really I am the last because he can't speak the Language. Those who do not speak the Language of the People are not truly the People. You study these things. Wouldn't you say that's true?"

"I think will I, yes."

She looked out the aluminum square of a window at the berry-stained mountains that she could not see beyond. Even now they had white on top that ran down in streaks like melting whipped cream. But the sun was high in the sky and warm and bright. "When he was very young, his name was Trees Standing Together and he spoke the Language. But it was about that time that all the leaders decided to give up their land and become a company like the white people. And because we were doing this it was thought to send all our children to white schools and Trees Standing Together became Bob." She chuckled a little to herself, still looking out the window. "Bob. And Bob cannot remember the Language. He bought me this 'trailer.'" There is no word for trailer in Kish'da y'k so she said it in English.

"His wife is from the Tlingit people down the coast. She speaks her language and he has learned a little. But I don't understand a word of it and their children will only speak English." She put her hands to her face and tugged as though her features were a hairpiece she was straightening. Then she picked up her long-handled wooden spoon, lifted the lid off the pot, and stirred a little.

"This a good to smell!" Dr. Krauss said cheerfully.

"He bought me this 'trailer,'" she said again. Then she giggled wickedly to herself. "I can't blame him. Who could he marry? His generation only had one girl. Six boys and one girl. I suppose one of them married her—Eaglefish. That's what she looked like. A nose like an eagle and two beady little eyes. Better to marry a Tlingit. Where did the other boys go?" she suddenly asked, as though she had never thought of this before. "They couldn't speak the Language either but I could make them the Soup. That would be good."

Dr. Krauss looked at her with sympathy. "Does Bob shout at you?"

She looked at him quizzically and so he tried again.

"Does he cry out to you?" Then he pointed at the telephone.

"Oh." She understood. "Call, we say. Does he call me? We are not ones for the telephone. He writes me. He and his wife have moved south to the lower states. He writes me. He writes."

"And who is he doing?" Dr. Krauss asked.

"Oh, he's fine," she answered and then thought better of her answer. "We don't have a language to write each other in. He can only write in English."

"And you can not English to read?"

She stared at him stubbornly. Then she got up and stirred her pot. "I can read it. But it is very slow. I once read a letter of his and it took three days' work. So I just answer him in English about how the seasons are changing. The snow coming and going and the salmon arriving and the bears coming down to fish them. And I thank him for the 'trailer.' What else can you say in English?"

"Where the letters to be found? I can help them to read you and then we can answer it together!"

She eyed him inch by inch, the way you eye a dog to decide whether it is dangerous. This was too much. What did this leader, this "doctor" want? She could let him practice the Language, though she was not clear why he wanted to learn a language that nobody spoke, that was leaving no written word behind, that would soon vanish when she did. But she would not let him into her letters. That was too much. "Well," she said tapping her thighs, "I would ask you to stay, but white people really don't like the Soup."

"Oh, but like I all things. I can to try?"

He stood up and she took her post by the soup as though to protect it from assault. "It is a fish soup but white people never like it."

"But you know how interest I be in all being from the People," he pleaded.

"Well, come see," she agreed with a friendly beckoning gesture and removed the lid from the pot while gently moving the soup with her wooden spoon. He looked in and to his surprise the Soup looked back up at him. In the milky churning broth were dozens of eyes, blind little eyes staring blankly, for they were cooked and cloudy. Salmon eyes seemed to drift around the broth in confusion and roll over, trying to look up, the way blind eyes do sometimes, seeking out light.

Dr. Krauss knew that he could not eat salmon eye soup and she had known that all along so there was no need for anything more to be said about it. They exchanged warm good-byes and he promised to "come be on top of you again" and she thanked him and he left.

She went back to the stove and lifted the wooden spoon to her mouth and sipped. It was ready. It tasted of her memory of Salmon Lady so many years before and Rocky Coast, who she missed, and sitting by the Lake of the People talking of things while skinning tough-hided animals. She opened a drawer and took out a stack of letters and ran her thumb along the edges. Most had not been opened. She placed them carefully on her table and ladled a bowl of the Soup and placed it on the table next to the letters. She looked out the window one last time because, strangely, in a trailer you could not look at the outdoors and sit and eat at the same time. The window was too high.

The sun was still in midsky. No darkness would fall this week. These were the long bright nights when they used to sit by the Lake and eat the Soup.

OSETRA

Often, later in his life, Wonderbread would recall as formative that instant when he first tasted osetra caviar. That was back when he brought caviar to the barrio.

The idea came from Masitas, who loved his masitas, little cubes of fried pork. After their friend Big Biscuit Rivera fell over, Masitas, Wonderbread, and Freddie Shalom realized they needed to do something for Mrs. Rivera. At first they lifted some cuchifritos but Mrs. Rivera didn't like cuchifritos—too fried, too greasy, too pork, and maybe just too barrio—and since they had taken it from Freddie's cousin's store, it could have been awkward if they were caught. But they were professionals—they didn't get caught. Still, Freddie Shalom didn't like the idea of hitting his own cousin, though he didn't like this cousin because a friend of Wonderbread's had opened his cash register and was now doing time. That was not the cousin's fault, but you could not expect Wonderbread to feel good about this man.

But that wasn't the problem. The problem was that Mrs. Rivera didn't like cuchifritos. She liked that Jewish stuff. So they put on their work clothes, Masitas and Freddie Shalom with their special double-lined coats and Wonderbread with his red and orange boxer shorts showing above his huge low-slung pants, his tight sleeveless shirt to display his tattoos, a stocking in red and white stripes and a single star, the Puerto Rican flag, covering his hair, and gold on every finger, each wrist and earlobe, sparkling at odd angles on his skinny chest like the torn-up chain mail armor of a battle-worn knight. A four-holed gold ring like brass knuckles spelled out the name Juan, which presumably was the name of its original owner. They were going to use "spic and spans" to get the stuff, but it was a game everyone in the neighborhood knew, so it worked much better in other neighborhoods. It would be perfect down on Broadway where the Jews lived, where that big Jew who visited Mrs. Rivera and left his card came from.

And so Masitas and Freddie Shalom browsed around inside, waiting for the entrance of Wonderbread, who played the spic, hitching down his pants and strolling into the famous Broadway store. Security spotted him immediately, as did many of the customers. While Wonderbread was being watched, Masitas and Freddie Shalom wandered the store, filling the inner linings of their coats—spanning—always being careful to make a distracting grab for the shelf with one hand while the other hand was smoothly slipping things in.

Security was on Wonderbread, accidentally bumping into him, brushing by him, stumbling against him. But they could find no stolen goods on him because he was stealing nothing. Meanwhile, the spans had three important covers. They never made contact with the spic, they never made contact with each other, and they always left separately. They would always choose some bulky but inexpensive item to stand in line and buy. In this case Freddie Shalom chose a dozen onion bagels and Masitas got the cream cheese.

They were also going to steal smoked fish, but they realized that they had to order it from a counter so that would not work well. Instead they found these little flat jars of caviar, which was also fish, and it was perfect because what you looked for in their trade was something small and expensive. But on a sudden impulse Masitas did something different. He saw a stack of boxes on a hand truck. What could be more normal than the sight of a young Latino wheeling away a hand truck? And so he walked out of the store wheeling four boxes—an espresso machine, two food processors, and a blender. They kept the blender to make batidos and sold the other three.

On the way to Mrs. Rivera's they picked up, literally, a papaya and a carton of milk. Triumphantly they entered her apartment and laid out the papaya and milk, the blender, bagels, cream cheese, and caviar on the table.

Mrs. Rivera inspected the goods, the new blender, the caviar, and she knew what had happened and insisted they take it back. Freddie Shalom became very wounded, which was evident from the expression on his face and his slow and persecuted rhythm as he reached into his pocket and produced a receipt for the bagels and said that he would try to find the other receipts as well.

Mrs. Rivera apologized and then apologized again and again. Then they set up the blender, added papaya, milk, ice, and sugar, and when it was cold and thick poured it in glasses, spread cream cheese on the bagels, and globbed caviar on top. It was a good thing they had gotten so many jars of caviar because there was not much in each one.

For Wonderbread, nothing was ever the same.

They had never tasted anything like this before. Masitas would always remember his first greedy mouthful of beluga. It exploded on his tongue—fragile, buttery bubbles of flavor, dark and rich as his mother's bacalao.

"Wait, bro," Wonderbread said, interrupting the eulogy on beluga. "Check out the osetra, bro. It just melts on your

tongue. Oh, man. And look at it. These things look like little gray pearls." His eyes were closed in an ecstatic trance.

"Like diamonds," said Freddie Shalom. "They sparkle,
man. *Por supuesto*, if we were paying for this stuff, I'd go for
the sevruga and save twenty dollars. . . ."

He realized that the other two were glaring at him.

"What? It's got more flavor and a better price." Then he
caught an odd look from Mrs. Rivera. "I mean if we were
paying full price. It was twenty percent off."

Mrs. Rivera looked pleased.

They ate everything and just had to do this again. More
bagels and caviar and batidos. They could get more caviar when they got more bagels and cream cheese. But the
caviar was small, easy to pocket, and sold for $70 for the
sevruga, $90 for the osetra, and $110 for the beluga. They
would take extra beluga to sell.

But the next time, while Freddie, Masitas, and Mrs. Rivera were enjoying their cold batidos and their caviar on cream cheese and bagels, Wonderbread sat quietly and ate a little jar of osetra by itself, with a spoon.

They went back down to the Jew store again. But now the caviar was kept behind a case and the customer had to ask for it. Those Jews were smart. It was obvious to professionals such as these three that once you asked for the caviar you were marked—you could not get out of the store without paying for it.

Discouraged, the three left. Masitas had had enough of caviar. It was not a good business and they needed to get back to the business. "Let's vamo'. We can't get fucked up on this caviar shit, bro."

"Hey, *pendejo*," said Wonderbread, silencing him with the point of a long finger with three gold rings gleaming. "We are entitled to lift the same food as anyone else. Don't you ever forget that." He dramatically moved his hands in a circular movement to his hips, hitched down his pants, and walked back in the store. Masitas and Freddie Shalom looked at each other. They only worked with Wonderbread because he made a good spic. He stood out. But he had no finesse for lifting. What was he doing? They stared through the window cluttered with rye breads.

Wonderbread got one dozen bagels. They even had papaya for the batidos. Then he walked up to the caviar counter and placed an order and was handed something in a bag—a small bag. Masitas and Freddie Shalom realized that he was only getting osetra, thinking only of himself, that selfish osetra-slurping motherfucker!

Then he moved out of sight for a minute and reappeared standing in line at the cashier's with no caviar bag showing and paid for the other items. Security grabbed him before he could get to the door. Outside Masitas and Freddie Shalom were clutching their legs to keep from running while inside the guards and the manager questioned Wonderbread and groped his body. Wonderbread did not stop them. He kept talking about "race profiling" and "unfair stereotyping." Wonderbread could talk. Eventually he had all three men apologizing.

When Wonderbread got out of the store he was smiling.

"Where'd you put it, bro?"

Wonderbread only smiled. Every now and then he would return to the store and eat another osetra. Where and how, the store never figured out. But sometimes they would later find an empty little jar on the back of a shelf somewhere. The store established a system where the customer gave the caviar order at the counter with a name and redeemed it at the cash register. No way around that one. Jack Milcher, the caviar man, hadn't wanted to do it. The thief was his only customer who knew the right way to eat caviar. All the others had their chopped eggs, pumpernickel, onions, and other atrocities. This thief appreciated it pure, the way it should be eaten. But he was costing the store hundreds of dollars and this was not amusing to the owners.

Wonderbread had to find a new store. Masitas always said, "Every time you go into a store you are taking a risk. Make sure you show a profit." But to Wonderbread, Masitas was a dull business type. Wonderbread saw more poetry in stealing. Sometimes he could find a store that felt safe keeping the caviar in an open refrigerator case. He could take a small flat jar of osetra and consume it unobserved in three orgasmic swipes of the tongue, pausing a second to let the little bubbles melt on his tongue, like lighter-than-air bacalao, he once said, and hide the empty container at the back of a shelf and walk out in a state of ecstasy. For Wonderbread, life without osetra had become unthinkable. And wasn't it right that something this good involved some risks?

CRÈME BRÛLÉE

Slipping someone you love a crème brûlée is a serious thing. Even if nothing happens you still have to live the rest of your life with you alone knowing what you did. For whom could you tell it to? Who would understand? Though when she thought about it, poisoning your lover was really nothing more than an extreme version of passive-aggressive behavior, so common to women trapped in overly protective relationships.

When newly engaged Emma left her family's Thanksgiving dinner, she was not even capable of conceiving of such an act. But what did she know of relationships? She had left the family dinner with only a deep sense that food was something that could not be trusted. The more she thought about this, the less she ate. She kept coming back to this idea of bean curd sealed in plastic. Shouldn't everything be? But then again why should you trust the people doing the sealing? Her fears became more extravagant in small, rational increments. She went from the idea that food should be wrapped to who does the wrapping to the need to eat food that was free of pesticides and chemicals, which led to a fear of food corporations to the decision to eat only organic to questioning if "organic food" could be trusted to be truly organic to the conclusion that no food could be completely trusted. How could a rational person refute any of these doubts? The problem was that it left her with nothing to eat. "I think we are too ready with complaint / In this fair world of God's," was a favorite quote of her father's. Browning. Elizabeth Barrett Browning, she thought. He would say it whenever she complained.

But it seemed to her that in God's fair world today, too little was known about the origins of most food. When she and Larry tried to plan their wedding she found all of the caterers profoundly untrustworthy. In fact, the more she saw of caterers—their discussions of finger food and spoon service and I can do a this and we could do a that—the more she wondered that anyone would trust them. After all, your only reassurance was that if their customers had regularly dropped dead from food poisoning, the outfit would have a bad reputation. But, she reasoned, once someone is dead, they can't really file a detailed complaint. And it is hard to know the cause when you have been poisoned. Especially with the amount of poison there is in food today—the pesticides in the earth, the heavy metals in the water, the vaccines in the cattle—each deadlier than the next. And all invisible. Who's to say which one got you? Now they were even warning about bottled water. Plastic bottles are poisonous. Food was really an endless hail of unseen bullets. Unseen and largely untraceable. The ideal murder weapon.

That startled her. She hadn't thought of that before. Suppose you had somehow offended some very unscrupulous person—scruples weren't exactly in fashion these days. Food poisoning was the perfect murder. You always hear stories of not very old people who inexplicably fall over. When does anyone investigate where they had been eating—had there been a friendly dinner with the ex or perhaps a business lunch? Wasn't it strange that people met over food and plotted to do each other in—financially, that is—and it never occurs to anyone that the competition might be getting the job done with the crème brûlée?

She was particularly suspicious of crème brûlée. How did the first crème brûlée come about? What was the chef trying to do when he accidentally burned the top? Isn't that carcinogenic? Has anyone ever done a study on the number of crème brûlée eaters among cancer patients? You see, no one studies these things.

She and Larry visited a baker to discuss the wedding cake and she simply pointed out that she had "reasons to be very wary of the health implications in the peculiar alchemy that makes cakes rise, etc." Just a simple observation. And what did the baker answer? She heard him say, "If you want, we don't have to have cake. We could do something like a crème brûlée, for example."

What? She could hardly believe what she was hearing. Though she should not have been surprised. After all, it was simply confirmation of everything she already knew.

"What did you say?" she asked quietly, hoping she had misunderstood.

"I said," said the baker, "that we could do a crème brûlée. That is, a number of them."

"A number of them?" asked Emma. "And which people would they go to?" she snapped like a lawyer who had just made her point in cross-examination.

"Whoever wanted them, I guess. Or something else. Chocolate mousse."

"Oh, that's just perfect, chocolate mousse. You could hide anything in chocolate. 'Seems a little bitter, my dear,' 'Oh, do you think so?' and then she dropped her head limp on her shoulder."

The baker was at a loss to respond. So was Larry, who said, "Why don't we continue this another day?"

He wanted to change the subject. That was peculiar,

Emma thought. He had been acting very suspiciously ever since they started planning the wedding, always coming up with strange people to bring in suspicious food.

All the way home Larry tried to defend crème brûlée, and when they got home Emma called off the wedding, called off the marriage, called off everything just in time and then realized that she was very hungry and went to the kitchen. She found a carrot and started to eat it and then remembered that it was a root. It grew in the soil. What soil? Isn't that dirt? What did she know about the soil where this carrot grew? She threw the carrot across the room—and happened to notice that it bounced. Wasn't that odd? Are carrots supposed to bounce like that?

She collapsed on the couch like the pile of sticks she was becoming, like a bag of golf clubs, and began to sob. How could she ever know what was safe to eat? How could she ever eat again?

Absentmindedly she picked up the television remote control and turned it on, drifting through the channels until half consciously she came to the Food Channel. She liked watching the Food Channel because there were lots of visiting chefs and food authorities and she liked trying to see which ones were a part of it, which ones were pretending to be lovely gourmets but were secretly involved in a conspiracy to poison.

At the moment Robert Eggle was on. She liked Robert

Eggle and had even bought some of his books. Maybe she could eat in his restaurant but she couldn't even remember what city it was in. But he was . . . he was cute. He had nice eyes and beautiful hair and the kind of hands you could trust . . . on your body.

She was going off in another direction. What was he saying? He was criticizing practices in "some of the leading restaurants." Then he said it. She could hardly believe her television. But he had said it. He said, "Take crème brûlée, for example."

"Yes!" she shouted out loud.

"If people knew what went on."

"Yes! He knows! He knows!" Emma was ecstatic.

"Did you know most of these restaurants melt the sugar with a blowtorch? A blowtorch!" he repeated for emphasis. "Soon they will be constructing wedding cakes with an arc welder."

"Yes!" she screamed. She knew what she had to do. She had to find a way somehow to meet Robert Eggle and then . . . and then she could eat again.

Robert Eggle had never intended to spend his life as an utter fraud. In truth he couldn't remember what he had intended but he was certain that this wasn't it. After he had left Margaret everything snowballed unpredictably down the wrong slope because of two, probably bad, decisions. He determined that until he had a better understanding of things he (a) would not tell anyone that he suffered from amnesia and knew nothing of his past and (b) would not reveal to anyone that he had lost his sense of smell and could no longer taste anything—that is, if he ever had been able to taste, but he must have, because he had a sense of it being missing.

Robert Eggle's new career began with the mystery surrounding his condition. At first, when dining with other people, because he seemed to find himself in some primitive culture where it was always necessary to comment on food, he limited himself to the observations for which he was qualified, such as "fibrous texture" or "a bread with the resilience of a marshmallow" or "a coldness that surprises." Occasionally he would venture into his elemental taste buds, with "an underlying bitterness" or sweetness, sourness, saltiness. His comments were always different from those of other people, always a bit unexpected and—more and more, it became noted—interesting.

His restaurant career was not an intentional fabrication but a desperate attempt to cover up. Don't many careers begin that way? Maybe this career was just one more thing he could not remember. When an interviewer erroneously stated that he had a restaurant in San Francisco, he did not have the slightest idea if he did or if he ever had, but he had learned to be a fast thinker and answered, "Used to." Interviewers always assumed that there was some reason they were interviewing this man. He continued with that answer, wherever it was suggested that the restaurant was located, and soon became the most celebrated restaurateur in America without having the ability to recall if he had ever had a restaurant anywhere. When in New York it was in Austin, Texas. In Boston it was in Portland, Oregon; in San Francisco it was in St. Louis; and in Chicago it was in Palm Beach, Florida. He could have easily been exposed, but there was no reason to be suspicious. Remarkably he had only one close call, when a New York food writer decided to fly to Austin to check out his restaurant. Sadly, Chez Robert had just closed in Austin but was expected to reopen "in some months" in Santa Fe, New Mexico. Everywhere he went he had a celebrated restaurant somewhere else and the fact that it was not rated or reviewed in anybody's food guide was further tribute to Robert Eggle's famously iconoclastic nature. He shunned food critics.

He had stumbled across the secret to success. Only by being closed can you be trapped. The person who is open to everything has endless possibilities. So when he received the note from the woman who wanted to discuss crème brûlée, he chose a quiet restaurant that he frequented with notables of the food world.

When Emma turned up, looking elegant, her soft, full

lips so different from her thin, bony body fitted into black silk, he was once again convinced that being open to everything was the secret of life. At dinner he discussed the little *amuse-bouche*, the appetizer, the aperitif, the first cold white wine—tasting everything before she did. In truth, she was waiting for him to go first but he didn't notice. This, she thought, was a man she could trust—a man who would protect her and taste her food. And so she decided to be honest with him.

"I was first drawn to you because I heard you on television and realized that you knew about the crème brûlée."

"The crème brûlée?" he repeated with a warm but uncertain smile.

"Yes." She leaned very close to him and tightly grabbed his hand and said, "That they were using it to poison people. But there are so many more things. They are everywhere. How do you know? I've been unable to eat anything at all."

In the first place, he liked the strength of her thin hand holding his and the hot moistness of her breath against his cheek. In the second place, Robert Eggle felt that he understood this woman, that she made more sense to him than most people he knew. He could understand fearing food and he could understand not wanting to eat it. In fact, it was a relief to be in the company of someone who did not want to eat. And even when he didn't understand her, he was used to that. He had learned to just go along with things. It was a natural disposition for a man who had no idea what was true and what was not or even who he was or what he could reasonably be expected to know. For a second he thought he should reward her trust with his own, clutch her hand and say, "I am a complete fraud. I can't even taste." But he could see that she was not looking for honesty; she was looking for support. He joined his second hand to the two that were already clasped and in all warmth and reassurance said, "Yes."

Tears welled in her eyes. "Yes?"

"Yes. It's everywhere and it's hard to know what to eat. You must be starving."

Her eyes could not hold the tears any longer and they were running down her cheeks. "Yes!" She smiled. "Yes! I am so hungry."

He ordered her course after course, always cautiously taking a first bite out of each dish, a first sip out of every glass. She needed him, trusted him, completely depended on him, and it felt . . . safe. Safe for both of them.

He took her home and she asked what she could eat for breakfast and he said that he would bring her breakfast in the morning and she told him not to leave. They were never apart again. He would bring her toast in the morning, buttering three slices and taking a bite out of each one. He sampled everything she ate, and she ate so much that for Robert, who was not really interested in eating, this sampling alone was all the nourishment he needed. On the other hand, Emma was looking very appealing two dress sizes larger.

Something about the way he took a bite from all of her food registered in most observers' minds as love. That was the way Emma saw it too. But she didn't talk about these things very much. After all, you never know who to trust. Except Robert. She could trust Robert. And that is all you need—one person that you can trust. To others the act of tasting seemed to have a touching intimacy. People would say, "Those two are so in love . . ." They never finished the sentence, which was a good thing because what sense would it make to say, "Those two are so in love that he samples her fettuccine"?

At their wedding, after the toast was made, Robert sipped Emma's champagne first and everyone applauded.

He never questioned Emma about who was poisoning whom or why, partly because he sensed that he was supposed to know already and partly because going along had always worked better than trying to understand. And they were very happy. Some things were understood. On several occasions they walked out of restaurants when they noted crème brûlée on the menu. And Emma was impressed with Robert's acumen when he caught one sly restaurateur concealing the crème brûlée behind the clever moniker "crema catalana."

It was clear to Emma why he was so celebrated as a food critic, commentator, and writer, why people read his books and articles. His website got as many hits as Foodofthe month.com and it didn't offer food. That was important to Emma because food purveyors were not to be trusted. Robert offered observations. "Nothing gets by Robert," Emma noted to herself with pride. Except that every now and then something did. There was a mocha mousse that he mistook for chocolate. If he could not detect coffee in the mousse, what else was he missing? And he failed to distinguish lime from lemon in a mayonnaise. These things were turning up after a few years of marriage, which was always when things have a way of turning up. But still, he protected her.

It occurred to Robert that Emma could be helped by seeing someone professional about her fear of poisoning. But he also understood that a cure would undo their entire relationship. He continued saving his wife from poisoning more than three times a day. She could not have a meal, not even a snack, without him. And so they were very close. He was always available for her, such as the time she was in a shop and a man threatened to demonstrate some kind of round branding device to be used in making crème brûlée. She called Robert immediately and he went to the store and got her.

To another man, some of these emergencies might have become tiresome but Robert loved being needed. And then something happened.

Robert had gotten an afternoon television cooking show. He had for years avoided getting into a position where his cooking skills would be tested. He did not even cook for Emma except for the simplest dishes such as toast in the morning. But when he was offered the television show for an extraordinarily large sum of money he realized something important about television: no one ever eats the food. And so he would invent outrageous dishes involving combinations such as herring, whipped cream, and graham crackers—Robert was into textures. As long as he threw the food around with aplomb, wielded tools with finesse, and garnished them on plates to look attractive, he was a success. Then one day, after having made green linguine with apricots, anchovies, cranberries, and a tapioca sauce—the colors were thrilling—Emma turned up for a surprise visit in the studio and to Robert's horror, while he was chatting with the producer, she stuck a fork into the linguine and was about to sample it—something she never did but she thought it would be in the spirit of television—good for her husband—and, of course, it was perfectly safe because Robert had made the dish. But in truth she did think it smelled a bit odd.

"Emma!" Robert whispered in what was more like a hoarse shout. When he caught her attention he shook his head negatively and Emma froze.

She had almost eaten it. But this was very peculiar.

Had Robert made poison? He saved her from it. Maybe even the people who made crème brûlée had families they protected. So . . . so, then . . . how was Robert any different from them? Wasn't he, in fact, one of them?

Though she said nothing about it, these thoughts filled her head. And almost absentmindedly she on occasion started to eat things without him tasting them first. The marriage was getting stale. Everyone noticed it. Sometimes the two of them would be seen eating from their own plates at a restaurant like a couple that had been married for years, like everyone else. They just didn't seem to be special anymore.

Then she ordered oysters.

In fairness, he did eat one of hers first but, of course, one oyster does not make you as sick as five oysters. Emma was five times as sick as Robert. Not only in her stomach and her head and with cold shivers through her body for three days—but in her heart. Robert had not detected the poison.

She began to secretly test him, the most daring test being the crème brûlée. She had to do it. Although she probably wouldn't have if she didn't feel so angry—so betrayed. While he was shooting his television show she went to a restaurant by herself and ordered fish, of all things, and ate it and seemed to be fine. For dessert she ordered . . .

Crème brûlée. Yes, she had deliberately gone to a

restaurant that made crème brûlée and dared to eat their fish. Then she carefully lifted a piece of the crème brûlée's dark amber burned crust—it made that suspicious cracking sound—and wrapped it in a napkin and put it in her purse.

The following morning while he was making the toast she slipped the crust into his espresso and stirred it until it melted. Robert could taste bitter and sweet and might have noticed if he hadn't added so much sugar. He liked sugar because he could taste it. But he could not taste the crust.

The crust seemed to have no effect on Robert but it changed Emma's life. Robert was a fraud. He could not detect toxins—not even crème brûlée. This should have driven her back to not eating but instead she began to eat almost everything. It just didn't seem to matter anymore. Robert could tell that he had been found out. When you spend your life waiting to be exposed, it is easy to recognize it when it comes.

"Robert," Emma said, "you have not been honest."

It was an intentional understatement. He knew that. And he knew what he had to do. He would tell her everything, the complete truth. She would be the only one who knew. He would trust her. It would be good to have someone he could trust. They would trust each other and share their own special secrets and the marriage would be back to where it had started.

"No, I haven't."

"Ever?"

"Since one day when I fell into a hole."

"What?" This was much stranger than she had thought. The best of marriages have their compromises and their secrets. Complete honesty is never a good idea. Now she knew that he was not to be trusted and though she tried to live with that, he couldn't. Robert could never bear having lost her trust. As for Emma, she never admitted having slipped her husband crème brûlée in his morning coffee and was always haunted by terrible thoughts of what could have happened. Come to think of it, why hadn't anything happened? There must have been something else that he wasn't telling her. They moved ever further apart until the distance was so great that the separation was almost painless.

He later heard that she had become involved with a politician. A politician. A man who they said might become a U.S. senator. Was this a man to be trusted more than a food writer? Robert wondered. But he knew the answer.

ESPRESSO

The house was so far out of town that it was hard to get there without a car. Yet one lone figure after another arrived on foot and walked up to the door. Before the skin of a knuckle could touch the oak on the door, Sandro would open it.

There was an awkward moment.

"Ciao, I am . . ."

"Rocco."

"I'm sorry?"

"Rocco, you're Rocco."

"Oh, yes, *mi scusi*. Rocco."

Sandro would take Rocco into the house and introduce him to his grandmother and the young man would start to give his name when the woman with the tissue-thin skin that barely concealed the fine bones of her face and the white hair wrapped up on top of her head would raise her hands, showing all ten delicate fingers, and cut him off. "It's Rocco."

"Rocco, yes."

"Don't worry about Nonna," Sandro would say with pride. "She has been in the movement about two hundred and fifty years." And his grandmother would lovingly swat the top of Sandro's head with a flick of the wrist. Then she would introduce the Rocco to a tall lean man with disheveled short white hair. His gray cardigan sweater had, near the third blue button, the kind of irregular hole that, it is said, an insect makes, though it looked more like a rodent took a bite out. He stared out at the world from deep-set eyes and had one of those long jagged noses that goes on with both the shape and rugged terrain of a Sicilian mountain crest. She would nod her head at him and say, "This is my new boyfriend," and everyone understood what she meant by "new"—that he was not in the movement.

With a thin, shaky, barely audible voice the new boyfriend would mutter, *"Lei vuole un espresso?"* and the Rocco would reflexively answer, *"Sì, grazie."*

"You can speak English," the grandmother would say, always very sweetly, though all the Roccos understood this as a reprimand. She was saying that the new boyfriend, not to be trusted, did not speak English. The Rocco would retire to the living room, a sloppy, comfortable room of soft stuffed chairs with worn rust- or olive-colored slipcovers, cobwebbed with white hairs that looked like they may have come from the head of the new boyfriend but more probably came from the flanks of the agitated little dog with some burning question in its eyes.

The new boyfriend would retire to the kitchen, where gurgles and hisses were released before the big sweep of a brass arm was lowered and a thick, chocolate-brown foam was squeezed into a tiny cup, filling it about a third of the way. Holding the saucer so that the little cup chimed as he carried it with an unsteady hand, the new boyfriend would bring the latest Rocco an espresso.

The latest Rocco would sit in a chair, sinking so far in that some question arose about ever getting out again, and sip his espresso. As he tasted the black froth, so bitter it filled all the buds on his tongue and sought out every corner of his mouth like a good masseuse working a back, he could feel himself rising out of the chair. By the time the cup was empty he was standing, pacing impatiently, and by then another Rocco was coming in. The first tried sitting down, beating out rhythms on the arm of the chair with fast-flicking fingers. Finally Sandro and all five Roccos were pacing the living room to the tintinnabulation of little espresso cups and the driving beat of fingertips.

When a Rocco finished, the new boyfriend would come in and take the cup and saucer, mutter, *"Un altro espresso,"* and disappear again. By their second or third espresso the discussion was progressing from whether to circulate an aboveground petition or an underground pamphlet. By now they were all pacing clockwise in a circle as if at any moment the music would stop and they would have to scramble for seats. But there was no music to stop and they kept pacing, one or two always tapping out a beat and the little white dog nervously studying the moving people, trying to understand.

"You have to do something to let them know the pamphlet is there," said one Rocco.

"Yes," said the Rocco in front of him.

A Rocco ahead of him in the circle added, "Like a bomb. A big bomb."

"What, are you crazy?" said Sandro, nervously fidgeting with his mustache.

A Rocca, who could not stop pacing to give her answer, said as she walked away from him, "You have to make a revolution to make a revolution."

"What is that?" shouted Sandro. "Are you quoting Che to me?"

Then came the porcelain jingle and the new boyfriend entered with a saucer in his hand. He looked concerned about the agitated expression on Sandro's face. He stepped very close and studied Sandro's troubled eyes for a few seconds. Then he said to him, *"Abbia un espresso,"* and he handed him the fresh cup; Sandro, still agitated, threw it down his throat like a shot of whiskey and handed back the cup, shook his shoulders as though throwing something off, and then said, "Or several bombs. That would get some attention."

"Yes," shouted a circling Rocco. "Coincidated throughout the city."

"Coincidated?" someone shouted.

"Whatever," said one of the Roccos just as the new boyfriend handed him a fresh hot espresso.

The fat overstuffed furniture was getting in the way of circulation and the Roccos were beginning to ricochet first off the furniture, then the walls, then each other, and the constant obstacles were contributing to their frustration.

"We have to make certain that no working people are killed."

"Bourgeois bullshit," said another Rocco angrily, not because it was bourgeois bullshit but because the other Rocco had abruptly bumped into him.

"The proletariat is the only revolutionary class."

"Oh, God," said another Rocco. "Don't start quoting Marx."

"It's not about classes. It's about freedom."

"Bakunin! That's even worse."

"Worse? Worse?" said a wild-eyed Rocca. "I cannot stand here listening to this anymore. I have to go for a walk." She marched to the door and then turned as though she just had a new idea. "You cannot create a revolutionary act without the underpinning of ideology. It is what separates us from thugs and criminals."

"Yes," said one of the Roccos. "But Bakunin, not Marx. This Marx is making me nervous."

"What's wrong with everybody?" she said and with that dramatically turned, doubtless planning to make her exit, but when she turned the new boyfriend was standing in front of her.

"Espresso?" he nearly whispered.

Uncertain, she paused, took the cup off the saucer, drank it down, said *grazie* as she put the cup back, her hand shaking, and left.

"I'm feeling very agitated," said one of the Roccos. "The cell can't be divided. I'm agitated. Maybe tomorrow." And he and another Rocco walked out the door. A third one tried to follow but was stopped by an espresso. The small white dog also looked very concerned.

How does he make them so quickly when he seems to move so slowly? thought Sandro, and he went into the kitchen where the new boyfriend was leaning over his work, his lanky body blue in the shadowy light, like a Picasso painting. The espresso machine was a large, complicated copper device with brass fittings resembling a nineteenth-century attempt at a submarine. The boyfriend brought down the long lever that pushed the brew through, turned to Sandro, and said, "America."

"What?" said Sandro.

"My boyfriend has a point. The Americans have forgotten about the Italians. They only care about Arabs," said the grandmother

"*Però*, Sandro," said the boyfriend, handing a small cup to Sandro, "America?" And he shook his head disapprovingly while clicking his tongue. *"Il caffè là è di merda."* The coffee there is shit.

Sandro carried his espresso to the living room, but everyone was gone. His hands were shaking; the chiming of the cup in the saucer annoyed him. He decided to take the dog for a walk.

MENUDO

There are waves that radiate from the fingertips, softer than electricity but just as powerful. Senator Jacob Green, head of the American delegation at the Latin American conference in Mexico, had his body overtaken by such waves. But all he said to himself was, "Five-hander."

The senator had a fascination with Mexico and like many people suffering from this nearly incurable fixation, he studied the Aztecs. He had learned of an Aztec king who measured women by how many hands it took to cover their pre-Columbian posteriors. Like the king, the senator always admired five-handers.

He had been working on his opening statement when his Spanish translator, Viridiana—he did not learn her last name—ran her fingertips in something between a caress and a massage around the senator's right shoulder. He wanted her to do it again. Uncontrollably his shoulder drifted in her direction. She did do it again. Subtly, or so he hoped, he bent into a quasi-Quasimodo posture as his right shoulder begged for more.

But then she walked away and that was when, though she was wearing a conservative, loose-fitting gray wool skirt, he made the assessment "five-hander."

It was a four-day conference. During those four days Senator Green, heading the U.S. delegation, felt an increasing need for Spanish translations, which came with those addictive electrical waves. He found an infinite variety of ways to offer Viridiana the right side of his body. His hand would move to her notes and she would lightly touch it, radiate it with swiftly passing digits.

At one point he managed to offer his shin, the straight lower part of his leg from knee to ankle. She found it, fitting her tingling radiating calf smoothly against the offering. . . .

By the end of the conference, though he could not close his eyes and tell you what she looked like, they had touched each other enough to have a secretive intimacy, the bond between two strangers who had slept together. Except that, of course, they hadn't. And that, as they both knew, was the unnatural thing about their relationship.

There was no discussion after the conference. The

senator had an engagement in Miami on Saturday and until then he was going to "disappear and study." He promised his aide, Roger Affel, that he would be available by cell phone. He called Emma, who for all her good points was a three-hander at best, and explained that he needed to stay there and work until the speech in Miami. Emma didn't question him because she was trying to learn trust.

Then they simply got into her little Korean car and drove away without discussion, like a couple going home at the end of a long workweek. They were not even irritated by Affel's three intruding phone calls, one about the upcoming Miami event and two about Washington matters. Roger was a nervous man, the senator thought. He sweated far too much to ever be in public office. He sweated worse than Nixon. And that was in Washington. He dreaded seeing him in Miami.

The senator did not even ask where she was driving. She was driving to a house, wherever that would be. She drove over the mountains to a green tropical plain. He did not even know whose house this was. She had arranged it, in a quiet Mexican village. Funny how in Miami he required security but here he was alone with his Mexican woman in a Mexican village. He had a tasty, boyish feeling that he was getting away with something not by being with this woman, which seemed a natural thing to do, but by skipping out on work, on security, by dropping out of the program for a few hours, maybe for a night.

And yet being with this woman in this Mexican village felt like what he should be doing. He had even mentioned something about "the translator" to Emma. Escaping observation was what was illicit, not the woman. For now he was just going home to a different life, a life he didn't know. A private jet would be waiting at the private airport, ready to speed him back to his real life. The story of who was paying for the jet was potentially far more explosive than the story of this Mexican woman and her house.

Soon they were in her home with embroidered bedspreads, turquoise walls, and an airy patio draped in greedily sprouting bougainvillea, both white and magenta. A pair of brown leather men's shoes was visible through a crack in the bedroom closet door. He did not ask. He had his own closets.

She removed his clothes methodically, as if preparing him for a bath. When he was naked he looked at her carefully for the first time. Until then, the touch of her hand and the vague curve of her backside had been enough for him. Now he could see that she was pleasant looking, not beautiful, youthful, not young, plumpish, not voluptuous. She removed her own clothes somewhat shyly, he thought, revealing cinnamon brown skin. She offered her body the way a mother feeds a child—generously, sweetly, selflessly, revealing no hunger of her own; the only desire was the desire to feed. He took it in turn the way a child takes food, thoughtlessly, selfishly, with deep satisfaction.

Later, on his cell phone, he reached campaign head-quarters in Washington. Everything could be moved until Saturday. Saturday in the synagogue in Miami Beach. This was what was known in politics as "securing your base" and that was considered essential. But until then, here was a small digression in a life that had never had digressions. After, the plane would be ready.

With Viridiana sex was not conquest but a calm physical expression of love. They went to bed by mutual assent.

And stayed there all night. The plane would be waiting.

In that first tangerine light of Mexican morning, he knew that he had to go. He dressed quickly. In his gray silk suit he was not hers and she sadly watched as his arms slid into the jacket, first one, then . . . then his cell phone played its little tune. It was Roger Affel, always a bit excitable, claiming that there was a security problem and he should delay his arrival. "What's the problem?" the senator asked in a cheerful baritone. He laughed when he heard they were checking a security lapse to make sure no one "poisoned the cholent."

A huge laugh from the senator. "That stuff's poison to start with." He folded up his phone and looked at Viridiana, soft and spice brown on the sheets. As he slid his jacket off, her dark face expanded, brilliant with the light of her smile. She got up and slid a hug around him.

"You're not going."

"Not yet."

"When?"

"Soon."

"First, I am going to make you menudo."

"Menudo?"

"You cannot leave until you have tasted my menudo. Promise me that."

The senator raised his long-fingered hand as though he were being sworn in by a court.

Viridiana skipped barefoot across the terra-cotta tiles to the kitchen. She reached into a canvas sack and scooped out great handfuls of corn kernels. The corn seemed like a balm, reassuring to her hands. She shoveled it into a brown earthen bowl and covered it with water. *"Bueno,"* whispered Viridiana and she went to her phone, an old phone, with a wire running into the wall.

Who was she calling? the senator wondered. It was still dark outside, still looked like night. But she was speaking Spanish, which of course he did not understand and which was why they had met. He did make out several times the word *importante*.

Back to bed, warm, cozy. The sun was bright when they woke up. Viridiana had put a robe on and gotten a package from the door, which she placed on the kitchen table and patted the way she might show approval to a spaniel. She hoisted the enormous earthen bowl of corn to a large pot and emptied it in. The senator could not help admiring how strong she was—a warm, soft, sturdy, dark body. She turned a flame on under the pot of corn, then, with the conviction of a broad jumper, skipped across the terracotta and leaped into the bed on top of him.

"You cannot leave until you taste the menudo," she whispered, snuggling into him.

He woke up probably only an hour later. Roger had not yet called. He felt like he was slowly climbing out of the deepest, most restful sleep he had ever known. Hearing the water running, he looked into the kitchen. Viridiana was naked, washing something in the sink, her fleshy dark Aztec posterior jiggling as she scrubbed. Why was he experiencing this kind of domestic peace that he had only heard of before now, somewhere in a green strawberry field, with a woman he didn't know—didn't need to know?

He quietly padded catlike across the tiles and knelt behind her. Placing a thumb on her right hip he began measuring with his outstretched hands.

"What are you doing?" She giggled.

Without rising he told her of the Aztec king.

"And?"

"I'm sorry. You looked promising but I'm afraid I have to send you back. You measured only four hands."

"Four of your big gringo hands," she protested. "Aztec

kings had fine, delicate little hands. I would easily have been a five-hander for him."

"You're right," said the senator from the floor with feigned remorse. He kissed her gently on her Aztec behind. Then he looked up and thought he saw large tears hanging in her eyes like two overfilled cups about to spill.

"Why?" he softly whispered as he rose to comfort her. But as she turned, he saw draped in her wet slick hands the slimy white and red entrails of some animal. He stepped back and as he did he tripped over a chair and crashed backwards onto the terra-cotta floor.

Suddenly the kitchen was filled with a little tune. The senator reached for his phone. He knew who it was. "It's chaos," Roger said excitedly as the senator stared at the drooping organs in the hands of Viridiana, who dared not move.

When he folded shut the phone she said softly, flatly, "Don't leave until you taste my menudo."

"What is that in your hands?"

His words freed her. They were not the ones she feared. "It's tripe and liver and over there is a foot."

"A foot?"

"A foot. You always need one good foot to make a menudo." She took them all and put them in another pot of water, then stirred the corn in the other pot with a wooden spoon, then turned to the senator. "You will leave and we will never see each other again."

"Oh," said the senator. "Is it time to start talking this way?"

"But it is true."

He took her hands, which he noticed were much smaller and more delicate than his. Aztec hands? "We will see each other," he said confidently. The senator knew how to persuade people.

"You will go to your wife and I will go to my husband and we will not see each other."

He knew better than to answer.

"You are the only man who has ever been nice to me."

He looked at her. Could this be true?

"Just don't leave until you have tasted my menudo."

"I'm not leaving," he said and sat on the chair he had tripped over. He knew he should leave but he had promised to taste the menudo. "When will it be ready?"

"Soon. But you cannot rush menudo."

She picked oregano from the window, chopped an onion, some garlic. She toasted three long, dried black peppers and crushed them. She roasted large dark green peppers.

The tune sounded again, horrid in its cheerfulness.

The senator walked away from her and she stood motionless as he talked. He knew he should have left hours earlier and did not know how he was going to explain this. What he wanted to say was, "The menudo is not done yet."

Viridiana could not hear what he was saying. Then he turned back to her with a smile on his face. Viridiana dared to smile back. The senator threw out his hands as though in helpless despair. "It's chaos. Chaos. The event has been called off."

She smiled happily as he embraced her. Then she pushed him off and went back to her pots.

Still, he would have to leave. With the event canceled, he should fly back to Washington. Back to Emma. He should call her. He looked up and caught Viridiana in her fleshy silhouette in the doorway, standing there reading his thoughts. With large, reproaching black eyes she said, "The menudo is not ready yet."

It took several more hours, most of the day, to make the menudo. Menudo takes time, but not a lot of attention. There were long, warm breaks when everything was left to cook. When it was done it was a soup the color of rich earth with bright yellow corn and honeycombed white meat. It was meaty tasting, spicy, burning just a little, giving almost every sensation a mouth can have. It had so many different textures and flavors that each mouthful was an unpredictable adventure. No wonder it took so long, the senator thought, to make all this. And for all those hours of cooking it was only minutes of eating. For years after, the senator remembered Viridiana and their short time in the strawberry fields together and when he did he always recalled that picante taste of rich menudo tasting the way life should be.

CHOLENT

This is how Senator Green was saved.

Rabbi Silberman was right about most everything until he said, "Cholent brings people together."

It was a small religious community. A few statistics tell a great deal.

Families that are paying members of the
    community: 130
Families that regularly attend High Holiday
    services: 130
Families that regularly attend Shabbat morning: 80
Families that regularly attend Shabbat morning
    when cholent is served afterward: 190

They would all come for any cholent. So would families from neighboring communities. There are many reasons why cholent is particularly Jewish and one is that no two Jews agree on how it is made. Every time a different family made the cholent it was a different dish.

"Cholent may not be good," said Rabbi Silberman, "but unlike most food, it has a reason to exist." Cholent is beans cooked with a wide variety of other things very slowly for a long time. Without the reason it would just be a bean casserole. Because observant Jews are not allowed to cook, to use fire, between official sundown Friday and official sundown Saturday, cholent was an opportunity for a warm Sabbath meal. You could start cooking it on midday on Friday and it could cook slowly to Saturday. They used to do it by putting a pot on a metal sheet that rested over a burner on low heat. Then the Crock-Pot—the long-, slow-cooking electric pot— came to Judaism. The community owned three and Harry Shapiro offered to contribute two more. "No small thing," he felt the need to add. "One hundred and fifty dollars each one."

"Five pots," reflected Rifka Sussman, "that's a lot of beans."

For a well-dressed woman, Rifka Sussman certainly knew her beans. She was a widow, though no one could remember her husband. Everyone would just shrug and say, "Who could survive Rifka?" She always had on a new dress with matching shoes and bag and one big visored hat or another that cast a dark shadow to conceal the aging process on her face.

Rifka's greatest skill was the art of the complaint. It was said that Rifka could find just the right complaint for any occasion. Once, after the death of one of the best-loved women of the community, ninety-four-year-old Leah Leben, the entire community was in tears and Rabbi Silberman, tall, elegant, and articulate as ever, gave a speech on the meaning of life that comforted everyone. When he left, the others talked of what a great man Silberman was, how he always had just the right words. "Such wisdom," one said. "Such compassion," said another. "But much too skinny," added Rifka Sussman.

As for Leah Leben, Rifka pointed out that "she bore her suffering like a fish."

"Like a fish?" said Minnie Mellman, who liked precision. She pulled her greenish blond wig down as though it were a bonnet and probed. "A carp? A tuna? A whitefish?"

"Like a fish," was all Rifka Sussman would say on the issue.

"Cholent is a dish with a reason," Rabbi Silbermen always said. It was best cooked slowly for twenty-four hours. The difficulty was that because of the Sabbath, it all had to be in the pot by sundown Friday. Jewish law did not allow any adjustments, any more work at all in the kitchen, until after the early evening service on Saturday, havdalah, marked the end of Sabbath. By lunchtime Saturday sometimes the cholent would be too dry because it had cooked too long or at too high a temperature. Sometimes it would still have too much liquid because it had cooked too slowly; sometimes the beans would be too hard and sometimes cooked to mush. But Minnie Mellman's beans were always perfect and her cholent had a sauce as smooth as chocolate. She always seemed to judge perfectly.

Minnie Mellman cooked the meat and onions and spices in one piece of cloth, vegetables in another, and beans in a third. Then all the pouches had to be opened up and mixed together. Rabbi Silberman said, "It shows that we start as individuals but we all come together in the end."

Harry Shapiro, who owned a dairy restaurant, seemed to lift Minnie's idea, separating the ingredients with layers of blintz dough, which some said was an advertisement for his own blintzes. Some said this was little more than a Jewish burrito, but Rabbi Silberman said that it was good to honor the Diaspora and they should remember the Jews of Mexico, whereupon only two weeks later Harry Shapiro proposed another cholent with corn and hot peppers, which he called Mexican cholent. Most of the community gasped in pain from the hot peppers, but this was in August near the time of Tisha B'Av and Rabbi Silberman said the suffering was good to remind people of Jewish suffering, although in truth they were supposed to remember Jewish suffering a few days later by fasting. Not eating is the usual way to remember Jewish suffering because normally Jews can imagine no greater suffering, but that is only Jews who have not tasted Harry Shapiro's Mexican cholent.

This spirit of openness and tolerance toward cholent ended when it was announced that Senator Jacob Green was coming to the community center next Saturday "to share in Shabbat."

"Senator Green," said Minnie with reverence in her voice.

"Yes," said Rabbi Silbermen with compassion. "Someday he'll be president."

"Or vice president," Rifka Sussman corrected. "He's not tall enough to be president."

Green was a Democrat whose name was often mentioned as a possibility to be the first Jewish president. Suddenly no one knew what to serve on Saturday.

"Maybe we should do cholent," suggested Minnie Mellman as though the idea had just come to her.

More than one hundred people were gathered in the hall where the reception was to take place. But above the assortment of kerchiefs, hairnets, yarmulkes, and black hats loomed the chiseled, bearded face of Silberman, a hat seated lightly on the graying crown of his head as though he were wearing it to appear taller, and with him, hatless with a close-cropped haircut that made the top of his head look like Velcro awaiting something to fasten to, was a tall, trim man in a black suit. Silberman introduced him as Agent Lemmon, in charge of security for the senator's visit.

"Okay," said Agent Lemmon in a commanding voice, "this is how it is going to work. You can make your soylent or whatever . . ."

"Cholent!" came back the angry correction.

"Okay. Let's keep it orderly. At eighteen hundred hours on Friday everyone leaves. We sweep the area."

"Regular Shabbas goys," Rifka Sussman offered. Some laughed.

"We keep the area sealed," said Agent Lemmon. "Saturday, twelve hundred hours, we start letting people in. We will have a list from Rabbi Goldman."

"Silberman!" the crowd shouted back.

"Sorry. The rabbi will give me a list of the members and those are the only ones who will be allowed into the reception."

At this the room filled with Jewish cacophony, so many people speaking at once so loudly that not a single word could be distinguished. Rabbi Silberman silenced them with three thumps of his palm on the table. Then, according to many, unfortunately, Harry Shapiro, who was not a member, spoke. "I don't need this. I was going to donate thousands to this community but . . ."

"I am sorry," said Rabbi Silberman. "But Mr. Lemmon is

mistaken. It is not a list of members. We are going to use the list of last year's Yom Kippur attendance."

"That's a go," said Agent Lemmon, reading from the top of the list. "It will be the Young Kipper list." He eyed the page suspiciously. Silberman then realized by the look on Harry Shapiro's face that he had also not attended High Holiday services last year. The rabbi had not noticed this at the time.

"So, I'm not so religious," argued Harry. "Does that mean I get left out of the cholent, when I bought the Crock-Pots, one hundred and fifty dollars each one? I am going to let this Agent Orange . . ."

"Lemmon," said Agent Lemmon in a cold tone. "And there is no need for that kind of thing."

"What kind of thing?" insisted Harry Shapiro. "Oranges, lemons. You think I can keep track? I used to ship all those fruits by the crate. By the crate!"

"The Florida oranges are not so hot. Better you should ship from California," Rifka Sussman pointed out.

Agent Lemmon passed a look of desperation to Rabbi Silberman, who stroked his beard an instant and then held up a piece of paper. "Everyone who wants to come, sign in and I will certify that I know you. I know all of you no matter where you *dovin*."

"I *dovin* where I like and I give where I like. That's just the kind of man I am."

"Don't worry, Harry," said Rabbi Silberman. "I'll put you on the list."

"But it can be no more than one hundred fifty people," cautioned Agent Lemmon.

"One hundred fifty families," Silberman corrected.

"No," said Agent Lemmon, "one hundred fifty people."

"We'll work it out," said Silberman, trying to quiet the room. "Maybe you could let in one hundred fifty for the senator and the rest just for the cholent after he leaves." This was met with a variety of noises indicating approval.

Agent Lemmon was amazed that this was an acceptable solution and he looked around the room suspiciously. "He will only be here for one hour," said Agent Lemmon, holding up a long and military-looking index finger.

"So maybe if it is such a quick visit we should just have some smoked fish," said Rifka Sussman. The crowd became angry.

"A warm meal is a mitzvah," said Rabbi Silberman, and Agent Lemmon directed his untrusting gaze on the rabbi. He did not like codes or secret languages.

"I could get a thousand dollars' worth of whitefish for three hundred," said Harry Shapiro.

"That too would be a mitzvah," said the rabbi.

"You see, and you were thinking of not letting me in."

"The whitefish won't be boned, like the last time?" asked Rifka Sussman.

"You don't bone whitefish," said Harry angrily. "I told you a million times nobody bones a smoked whitefish."

"Someday someone will choke," was Rifka's stubborn final word on the subject.

"One hour," repeated Agent Lemmon. "He comes in from Mexico. Then leaves for Washington."

"Mexico!" Harry shouted. "Then I am making Mexican cholent." The crowd began to protest. But Harry insisted. "When you come back from vacation it is always nice to taste something from the local cuisine."

"The local cuisine is *treif*!" declared Rifka Sussman.

"Is Senator Green kosher?" asked Minnie Mellman.

"Well, my pot is going to be Mexican cholent," Harry insisted. "Kosher Mexican. That will be a mitzvah." Agent Lemmon shined his blue stare at Harry. He apparently did not like this word "mitzvah."

This left four other pots to fight about.

"I could make a duck cholent," said Naomi Weinstein.

"Duck!" came back the outcry.

"With oranges," was the soft-voiced defense of Naomi Weinstein, who had always felt a little too chubby to be assertive.

"It's French," declared Harry Shapiro, always an authority, despite his enormous paunch that made it look like he was about to give birth to a prehistoric creature.

Men are so lucky, thought Naomi, who had dieted all her life.

"And why would French be good?" asserted Rifka Sussman, pulling her linen jacket down from the bottom as though to remind people that her full figure had once been impressive. "Anti-Semitic sons of bitches."

"I went to Chez Bernice once," Naomi Weinstein added, hoping it might help.

"And they had cholent?" challenged Leonard Zipkind, the skinniest man ever to run a candy store.

"Don't be ridiculous," said Rifka Sussman, adjusting the tilt of her broad-brimmed hat. "Even if they did make cholent, they would call it cassoulet and fill it with all kinds of *treif.*"

"I went to Chez Bernice," declared Harry belatedly. "I dropped more than five hundred dollars there. And I've had better food."

"Since we are doing Mexican," said Rabbi Silberman, "it would be good to do French as well. Cholent symbolizes bringing together and, after all, Senator Green is a man of international interests."

"Well, if he is such a liberal, I can make vegetarian," said Minnie Mellman.

"He's a vegetarian?" said Harry Shapiro.

Rifka Sussman pointed out that vegetarians have sodium-poor diets. "They get thinner and thinner and eventually they faint."

But no one argued with Minnie Mellman about cholent. Tsipora Yehuda was a different case. She could not make cholent. Whatever kind she attempted, no matter how much water she added, what heat she left it on, by the midday meal on Saturday it was as dry as unused clay. "What is your secret?" she would always ask Minnie Mellman, who would pull down her wig and not answer because she knew Tsipora's secret. All the men always wanted Tsipora to come with one of her cholents, even a dry cholent, because Tsipora Yehuda was beautiful. She had black curly hair and she showed it. Nor did she hide a well-shaped, fit young body and an Israeli accent that made everything sound slightly more exotic, even when she said, "O', it is dry-ed again."

"But the flavor, oh, the flavor. Flavor is what matters in a cholent," the men would all insist while Minnie listened in angry silence.

The last pot was claimed by Leonard Zipkind, who put chocolate in everything. For Passover his chocolate-covered macaroons had long been popular and for the New Year he had chocolate-covered apples. But this year stranger things started appearing, such as the chocolate chip potato latkes for Hanukkah, liked by only a few, and now the chocolate cholent was awaited with a certain amount of dread, not helped in the least by Harry's reassurance that Mexicans always put chocolate in their stews, which was followed by Rifka's assertion that "Mexican food gives everyone the runs."

The list proved even more difficult. It was fought over name by name. When names came up that were not on the membership list Rabbi Silberman would pat Agent Lemmon's shoulder and say, "Let them come. It would be a mitzvah."

Agent Lemmon narrowed his eyes and studied the tall rabbi in the long gray coat.

"A good deed. A kindness."

"Sure. Let them in," Roger Affel, the senator's chunky aide, who had one side of his face permanently concealed by a cell phone, would say. At first everyone had laughed because they thought Affel's name was Apfel, which means apple. "Fruit," said Minnie Mellman. "They all made up fruit names. Lemon, Apple, soon Doctor Plum will show up."

"Not such a joke," said Rifka Sussman. "They are all undercover."

"Do you know what it costs to change your name?" pointed out Harry Shapiro. "I wanted to be"—and he said this with a special lyricism—"Tony Shepherd. But the cost of changing? Forget it."

Friday afternoon the five Crock-Pots were filled and bubbling; the other cholent makers had watched Minnie Mellman to see at what temperature she set her pot, how much water she had in the pot, how she made her cholent perfect. Minnie had unceremoniously filled the pot, set it on low heat, straightened her greenish blond wig, and was standing by the candelabra with the beautiful Tsipora Yehuda waiting for the moment to light the Shabbas candles, which would also be the moment when all cooking had to stop.

Agent Lemmon and the Secret Service cleared everyone out of that part of the building. Soon the Sabbath worshippers had gone home for dinner. In time the Shabbas candles burned out one by one and the large reception room was dark except for five orange lights, like animal eyes in a blackened forest, glowing from the Crock-Pots. There Agent Lemmon passed the night with five eyes staring at him in silence.

Shabbas morning began tumultuously. During the night Minnie Mellman had entered the cholent room, not realizing that Agent Lemmon was there. Fortunately, he intercepted her before she could touch the Crock-Pots or the cholent would have been hopelessly compromised. No one could be allowed to tamper with the food. There was still some uncertainty in security. He had approached her in the dark, apparently taking her by surprise, and she dropped a plastic pitcher filled with what appeared to be water. Lab analysis quickly confirmed that it was only water—tap water—and security was satisfied.

Even before morning services had ended, people started gathering by the door to the reception room. Agents had a list and demanded identification. Many of them were not on the list and, though sent away, stood by the doorway shouting such phrases as "There's cholent cooking," and "They have cholent," and "I can smell the cholent," and "But I always come for the cholent," all of which fused into an inaudible roar.

Then Harry Shapiro took a spoon and dipped into the beautiful Tsipora Yehuda's dry cholent and smacked a heavy wad onto a paper plate. "I'm trying some of Tsipora's," he said flirtatiously.

"I wouldn't," said Tsipora indifferently.

"Please, wait!" said Agent Lemmon.

"Oh, how bad could it be?" Harry Shapiro reprimanded.

It was too late. Now everyone was struggling toward the five pots—or four, because everyone new about Tsipora's cholent. It occurred to some that Minnie Mellman's might be *treif* but one look at Tsipora's and the Mexican and the chocolate and all suspicion was lifted from Minnie Mellman, whose cholent was first to go.

"What are we going to do?" said Agent Lemmon to Roger Affel. "They've compromised the cholent."

Roger smiled. "Well, I guess if no one drops dead we'll know it's not poison," said Affel, moving away from the crowd to use his cell phone.

There were moans of ecstasy. Then Rifka pointed out, "Good, but this kind of food will kill you."

That got Agent Lemmon's attention briefly until Minnie Mellmen started fighting her way to the pots, shouting, "*Ayn bebel!* Just give me *ayn bebel*," pleading for one bean. Another argument about cholent recipes was bubbling. Several, though of course Rifka was first to point it out, thought that Minnie Mellman's cholent was dryer than usual.

"Dry. Dry, dry. I couldn't charge five dollars for this," Harry Shapiro pronounced.

"You've charged ten dollars for worse," shot Rifka.

"That's why I don't serve you in my store anymore," Harry said, his voice growing even louder.

"Somebody has to say something if the food is not good!" Rifka shouted angrily.

"But it's always *after* you've eaten everything, you *chazzer*."

"I'm a *chazzer*? Only one time I'd eaten everything before I complained. Only one time!"

"*Hak mir nit in kop*, Mrs. Sussman. Stop banging my head, will you? Three, maybe four times you ate everything, then you complained."

"Twice at the most," Rifka Sussman protested.

Lemmon said to Affel, "We can't bring him in with this kind of chaos." But Affel was on his cell phone. It was still early in the day; the senator had a short flight. Sundown wasn't until late. Not sure of what to do, Agent Lemmon walked over to Tsipora Yehuda's pot, where there was no line. Then Tsipora got his attention with her dark and beautiful eyes. She shook her head no and presented him with a plate of Minnie's cholent. He tasted it. And immediately felt satisfied. Even if it wasn't his culture, there was something so warming, so filling about this food that it made you feel safe, protected. It reminded Lemmon of his mother's pork and beans.

"Do you like it?" she asked.

"It's great! It's like old-time pork and beans." Immediately Agent Lemmon wished he hadn't said that because Tsipora Yehuda was so beautiful. "Tsipora is a beautiful name. What kind of name is that?"

Tsipora stared back with a look he understood to mean, What kind of name do you think it is? But she took pity on him and instead of saying, It's a Jewish name, what did you think? Hotentot? she said, "It means 'bird' in Hebrew."

"What a beautiful name," Agent Lemmon declared, and Tsipora smiled politely, having already known that it was a beautiful name.

Affel made an apologetic announcement that the senator was not going to be able to make it and there was a groan of disappointment. Then some went back for more cholent.

Soon all that was left in the room with Agent Lemmon were five empty pots, a garbage can of used paper plates, and Rabbi Silberman. Agent Lemmon shook his head and walked up to the rabbi. "What happened?"

Rabbi Silberman said, "Havdalah. They've gone to pray."

"Are they coming back?"

Rabbi Silberman looked at the empty Crock-Pots and shrugged. "Shabbat will be over. They can go home and cook. Cholent is a food with a purpose."

BOUDIN

One of the only certain facts that everyone knew about Andy Ledoux was that he was a liar. In the ten years he had lived in the parish he had told so many lies that no one was certain of anything else about him. Was his name really Andy Ledoux? Was he from New Orleans, or "New Oilins," as he said, with an accent that identified the exact ward he came from but which sometimes vanished in the heat of conversation? Some didn't think he was even from Louisiana. He might not even be from the South. Despite his repeated stories about his childhood on a Louisiana plantation, there was a rumor he was from Wisconsin.

He was supposed to be dating Chancy Maire. They were always being seen together. But he had told her and everyone else that he was engaged to Madonna—yes, the pop star. No one really believed it and Madonna never came to town. Sometimes he would talk about other women he had met in New Oilins and someone would snidely ask, "What about Madonna?"

He would either ignore the comment, saying nothing at all, or he would say that Madonna understood these things, that they had "an arrangement." Chancy did not worry about Madonna and in time Andy announced with gravity that they had "broken up."

Andy did not put much effort into explanations. Telling the story was all that was important. If confronted with an obvious lie, as when Petey Michoux actually went to the famous plantation off the bayou in New Iberia and confirmed that Andy had never lived there and then bullied a historian back in town into denouncing him, Andy would just shrug and not answer. He never defended his stories. He just didn't care if you believed him or not. And that made people a little uncertain about what otherwise would have seemed to be obvious fabrications.

There was one other certainty about Andy. He was a great charcutier. His spiced pork, bacon, tasso, sausages, boudin blanc—he wanted to make boudin rouge but it wasn't allowed by Louisiana law since someone had died from it—his andouilles, his smoked brisket, all his pork specialties were the best anyone in town had ever tasted, and these people were pork connoisseurs. Some said he had named himself Andy after his celebrated andouille sausages. Someone from Wisconsin couldn't cook like this. His food was so good that some people even believed him, despite their better judgment, when Andy announced that he had gone into partnership with Robert Eggle, who wanted his help to start a Cajun restaurant in town.

It was possible. Andy made great food and Eggle had started famous restaurants just about everywhere else. This could mean a lot to Verport, a slightly cursed little town of mosquitoes that had been founded by a man who couldn't spell in French and so what should have been Greenport had a name that meant "wormy port," or as the locals liked to call it, "Worm Town."

With a famous restaurant coming, everyone started fixing up Worm Town, once again completely forgetting to doubt Andy. Houses and fences were getting painted, and a traffic light was even installed at the main intersection where cars had been colliding about once a month for at least a generation. The mayor tipped off the Immigration and Naturalization Service that there was reason to believe that Mexicans were being landed in the bayou. He didn't want illegal aliens panhandling the restaurant customers. That irritated Sheriff Omar Grimley, because he hated federal agents. "Who the hell would land illegal Mexicans in the bayou?" he snarled and spit. "Hell," he said with a malicious chuckle, "it's too dangerous with all the South American drug dealers in there."

Sheriff Omar, as everyone called him, fiercely guarded his terrain, thinking he had to be assertive because he was too small and certainly too skinny to be a real southern sheriff. He knew he was not just imagining this, because his gun belt cinched to its last hole barely stayed on his hips and he always felt like its weight was going to cause his baggy pants to fall to his ankles at an unpropitious moment. He ate in his patrol car most of the day, starting with a cup of gumbo for breakfast and moving on to oversized po'boys, oyster or pork, that squirted mayonnaise when he tried to get his small mouth around them. But he never widened an inch.

The mayor also called in federal drug agents. "With tourists coming in foreign cars to eat fancy étouffée at the restaurant, we can't have shoot-outs down on the bayou," he said, failing to explain why there would be such an occurrence since there never had been before. To Sheriff Omar's satisfaction the cocaine always landed quietly and peacefully without any disturbances.

Suddenly a budget appeared for street sweepers, which no one had ever seen before in Worm Town. Everyone thought it was a good idea but no one wanted the job, forcing the town to hire Mexicans.

It was winter, not long before carnival, but it was

already getting too warm, the warmest winter anyone could remember. "Enjoy the global warming," said Andy to Artie Hagstram, while wrapping up sausage, and then he went on to explain about the machine he had invented that they were using in Greenland for measuring glaciers.

"Just tell me when Madonna's coming," said Artie in an unkind tone as he pushed open the screen door that was already needed to keep out mosquitoes.

"Sure will," said Andy, unfazed, his somber and somewhat aloof face turned to inspect the glass counter where his sausages were stored. He then opened the stainless steel door to his refrigerator, took out a package, untied it, unwrapped it, and peeled off a translucent sausage casing to wash out one more time before using it.

Chancy came in. "Afternoon, Andy."

"Afternoon, *cherie*," said Andy. The way he called everyone *cherie*, the slightly off tone of it, was one of those little things that convinced some locals he was a Yankee posing.

Andy was squeezing water out of a casing and holding it over the sink in a way that Chancy could not help but think looked like he was urinating. All the Worm Town men pissed in the bushes on their way home from Casey's late at night. It was the kind of crude thing that Andy didn't do. That was what she loved about Andy. How different he was from the other men of Worm Town, which was most of the men she had ever known. He was more refined, more sensitive, kinder. So it made her laugh to watch him by the sink with the casing. His hands were always so pink and white, like the raspberry Creamsicles she used to love. She guessed that was caused by his hands always being in water—the cleanest hands in town.

"Everybody sure is cleaning up old Worm Town," said Chancy.

"They better, *cherie*. We are bringing them a three-star restaurant. I personally assured Mr. Robert Eggle that Verport was ready for it." Andy and the mayor were the only ones that ever called Worm Town "Verport."

"Three-star. And we are going to do a cookbook. The *Verport Cajun Cookbook*. We have a contract from New York. And there is going to be an introduction by Tennessee Williams."

"Isn't Tennessee Williams dead?"

"That's true enough, *cherie*," said Andy, without a change of voice and offering no further explanation. "I was with him when he died," was all Andy added, which, of course, clarified nothing.

She wanted to ask him about knowing Tennessee Williams, but, like everyone else, she knew that he often lied and it saddened her and so she avoided questioning him on his statements for fear it would encourage him to lie further.

"Here. I'll show you something, *cherie*," said Andy as

though he had heard the question she had decided not to ask. He opened a cabinet under the cash register, squatted down, rummaged inside, and came back up with a small thin black wooden picture frame, which he handed over to Chancy. It held a black-and-white photo of two men— one short and one tall—in what seemed to be matching white linen suits. The shorter man with the mustache was unmistakably Tennessee Williams. The taller, clean-shaven one, younger but just as somber, was unmistak-ably Andy Ledoux. His face was fresh and lean. He looked like Andy's teenage son. Andy thought the picture would answer a question, but for Chancy it had the opposite effect. She wondered when the picture was taken, if it had some-how been manipulated, but if so why would he have shown himself that young, and why as only a teenager would he have known the famous writer? On the other hand, maybe this was the proof that he really was from the South. It was astonishing the way he could do that—come up with just a few verifiable unlikely truths so that you could never be sure he was lying.

"How did you know Tennessee Williams?"

"We had the same director."

"Director? You were a playwright?"

"I wrote the book to *Oklahoma*. Then I got cheated out of the credit. . . ."

There he went again. She wanted to stop him. "Where's

the new restaurant going to be?" she asked, to force him off the subject.

"As soon as Robert Eggle gets here we are going to pick an appropriate venue."

"Do you want to go to a movie or something tonight?"

"You know I would love to, *cherie*. But Robert Eggle is coming in tonight. I have to wait for him."

"Tonight?"

"Yes, *cherie*."

It was always like this. She asked him out because he never asked her and then there was always some excuse. It used to be that he had to meet Madonna. Now it was Robert Eggle. Well, if he knew Tennessee Williams, he could know Robert Eggle and maybe even Madonna. But not all three. She angrily swatted mosquitoes as she walked home on the freshly swept sidewalk. It was warm for January.

"It's a warm winter night, *cherie*," Andy called after her. "Enjoy the global warming."

Suddenly a large black pickup truck with an engine that purred with the deep resonance of a large jungle cat came up behind her. She didn't have to look. It was Petey. "Get in. I'll give you a ride."

Defeated, she obeyed, climbing up and into the truck.

"What's the matter, your girlfriend left you for the evening?"

"Shut up, Petey."

"There's always me, if you get tired of fairies."

She crossed her arms and refused to look at him. "Are you driving me home? It's right here."

He reached over and opened the door for her. "What are you going to do, spend your evening pining away for some tinkerbell who's out cruising for little boys? That's what they do. Find little boys, drag them down to the bayou, and have their way with them."

"That's disgusting."

"I know."

"The truth is this town's too backwards to appreciate a man who spends his evenings doing anything besides getting drunk at Casey's. A man who's known people like Tennessee Williams."

"I bet. Wasn't he another one?"

"Why's everyone in this town have to be so backwards?"

"'Cause it's Worm Town, darlin'," Petey said, laughing, as he closed the door and drove off.

By daybreak, Sheriff Omar Grimley was in an irritable mood. He had been up half the night, sucking strawberry Dixie Freezes through a straw until the Dixie Freeze closed, harassing everyone who left Casey's for being drunk. He was supposed to arrest them, according to the mayor, but he just said, "If you're going to be drunk could you just stay off the street so I don't have to deal with you?" He was irritable because the Dixie Freezes lolled cumbersomely in his belly yet he knew they would not fatten him, would not give him a gut to hang his gun belt on, and the later it got the more it felt like the belt would slip past the Dixie Freezes and pull everything down to his shoes.

He was also irritable because wherever he went he saw federal agents out of the corner of an eye, just watching him, hoping he would lead them to something. Sheriff Omar didn't see anything, he didn't want to see anything, and he had resolved if he did see anything he would act like he didn't rather than give them a tip.

So in the early morning with the gray fog still rising from the ground, when Sheriff Omar did see something a little curious, he deliberately didn't react. A dusty beat-up pickup stopped at the garage next to the charcuterie. Neither the truck nor the sinewy white-haired man who drove it was from the parish. Omar believed that the singular invaluable skill that he brought to his work was his ability to identify who was from the parish and who wasn't. This man clearly wasn't. Andy Ledoux, who lived in an apartment over the garage, came down with a package wrapped in paper and tied up with a string and handed it to the stranger. The man handed money to Andy Ledoux and took the package and left. Sheriff Omar looked furtively to both sides and saw no federal agents in sight, reached in his bag for a chocolate-covered marshmallow pinwheel, and kept driving.

Chancy wondered what Andy Ledoux did with his evenings instead of taking her out. Robert Eggle had not come to town, an obvious fact that was not in the least bit awkward for Andy. He was very adult about things and she was going to be adult too, she told herself. That evening Chancy positioned herself in the bushes where the shrubs turned into a weeping, moss-strewn forest that led to the bayou. It was dark and it was all blackness except for the light in the charcuterie. By the time that light went out, the mosquitoes had arrived, but Chancy didn't dare move. Why were there mosquitoes in January?

Andy closed his shop, turned off the lights, and walked toward the dark woods, still wearing his white apron that he had worked in all day without getting a single spot on it. Even without any light around it, it seemed to glow.

Where was he going? Chancy wondered. He seemed to be heading into the bayou. Was Petey right? Was he going there to meet little boys? That was ridiculous. But a lot of people in town said that he was a "homersexshul." They had a way of pronouncing the word that made it sound classical Greek. Maybe tragic.

Chancy started to follow him but she couldn't find him

and, tired of being in the mud and tripping on roots, and harboring a lifelong fear of alligators, especially in the dark, she went back and waited under the bush. No one would go in the bayou at night without a very good reason. Soon she fell asleep and only woke up when the mosquitoes started biting her at first light. She could hear birds, some crooning, some chirping, a few squawking down by the black water. There was no light on in the garage or the shop. Was Andy still down there? Was he all right? He wasn't from the bayous and to outsiders it can be impossible to tell land from water because of the thick vegetation. There are entire islands where no water can be seen around them but a local with a pirogue can completely circumnavigate the land.

Emerging from the bush she heard that deep-chested purr again of Petey's pickup truck. "Out kind of early, aren't you?"

"Aren't you?" snapped Chancy.

"Darlin', this is when I go to work."

Chancy silently prayed to unknown gods that Andy would not emerge from the bayou at this moment.

That's the problem with unknown gods.

"Holy shit!" said Petey. "What the hell has he done?"

Andy was coming out of the darkness like some sort of primordial amphibian. His gray pants legs and shoes were layered in blackish mud. He was carrying a bucket, and his

Thank You
for Your Business!

Thank You
for Your Business!

Thank You
for Your Business!

Credit Card Purchase --
        Maple ST Book Shops
     7523/29 Maple ST, NOLA 70118
     (504)866-4916(new)/7059(used)
     www.maplestreetbookshop.com

3/18/2013 11:47:53 AM   Invoice # 83667
Cashier ID: 01
Station ID: 2
# of items: 2

(USED) The Story Sisters
9780307393869 1 @ $12.00 $12.00
(USED) Edible Stories: A Novel in Sixteen Parts
9781594484889 1 @ $6.00 $6.00

Sub Total $18.00
Sales Tax1 Total $1.62
Grand Total $19.62
XXXXXXXXXXXX

hands, his forearms, and his apron were a kind of bright clay red, dyed by something that could only be blood. He was dripping in blood. He looked at no one and made his way into his shop.

As Chancy turned to look at Petey she saw the sheriff in his car across the street sipping on a cup of gumbo, looking in the direction of Andy and showing no particular reaction to anything. Petey got out of his truck and ran up to him. "D'you see what I seen, Sheriff?"

"Don't know what you saw."

"I think that faggot's taking little boys down the bayou and killing them. God, doing something awful."

Sheriff Omar took a paper napkin and wiped the corners of his mouth. He looked to the right. Then he looked to the left. Then he looked at Petey and smiled. "I think you're mistaken."

Petey pointed at the place where he first saw the blood-soaked Ledoux emerging. Chancy came over and asked, "What do you think it is, Sheriff?"

"Jeez, what are you doing here?"

"Petey's got some weird obsession with little boys," Chancy blurted out.

"It's not me that's got the weird obsession," Petey said.

"Listen," said the sheriff in nearly a whisper, "I don't know of any little boys missing. Do you? Now look, I think it would be a lot better for the town, especially with this fancy restaurant coming in, if I could just handle this without all those federal boys the mayor called in. You know what I mean? Now if you can just be quiet about this I can tell you what's going on."

Who could pass up that offer? They both agreed to secrecy. The sheriff leaned out of the car and in a hoarse whisper croaked, "Drug deals going down here. I've been watching it."

"But whose blood is it?" Petey demanded.

"Well, I figure since there's no one missing and since I personally have seen the goods change hands and it's always people that aren't from around here he's dealing to, I figure if he did in one of these Mexican boys who runs cocaine up the bayous here, nobody's going to know the difference. They're not going to be reported missing. Nobody knows them, right?"

They both agreed and Petey drove off to work and Chancy walked back home, trying to conceal the tears that were sliding from the corners of her eyes, and neither of them felt satisfied with Sheriff Omar's explanation.

Chancy knew she should stay away from the charcuterie but she couldn't.

"Hi, there, Andy," she said with a little too much cheer.

"Afternoon, *cherie*," said Andy Ledoux with his customary somber voice. He was at the sink scrubbing the dark cuticles of his fingers where the blood would not wash out.

Chancy watched him in silence for a moment. "Want to take in a movie tonight?"

Andy was still concentrating on his fingers and Chancy had a quick flash of panic. What would she do if he said yes? But he didn't. He quietly said, "I can't tonight, *cherie*." He said it just as though he had never said it before.

"Robert Eggle?" Chancy suggested tauntingly.

"Yes, that's right. He's coming tonight. We have to pick a venue."

Chancy felt jolted with a realization that shot straight into the stomach instead of the brain. She walked out of the shop without saying another word, which Andy Ledoux in his calm way did not even seem to notice as he continued to scrub his fingers.

"I don't believe it's a Mexican at all," said Petey. "Unless it's Mexican little boys."

"You and the little boys. There's none missing!"

"Not from here. He's getting them from somewhere else. Maybe they are Mexican."

"Petey, I figured it out. I know who's missing."

"Who?"

"Robert Eggle! He's killed Robert Eggle!"

"Who? Eggle? That restaurant guy?"

"Yes! What are we going to do?"

Chancy was afraid of what would happen to Worm Town when they found out that there would be no restaurant because Andy had killed Robert Eggle. She told no one. But the next morning she and Petey and several other people saw Andy Ledoux emerge from the bayou again covered in blood. By noon everyone in town knew.

"Son of a bitch!" Petey shouted at Chancy. "He can't be killing Robert Eggle every night, can he now?"

Chancy silently shook her head.

"And he can't be killing a different Mexican drug dealer every night. Hmm? He's getting little boys and we're just standing here letting it happen. Well, I'm not going to. I'm getting the son of a bitch tonight. The hell with the sheriff."

"Let me just try talking to him."

"Oh, yes. I can see that. I'll tell you what. You go talk to him and if you can find some explanation come and tell me. Otherwise I'm taking care of the son of a bitch tonight."

And so Chancy went to the charcuterie again. There were no customers because everyone had heard.

"Andy," Chancy pleaded, "you're not meeting Robert Eggle. We can see that."

"I met with him last night. I told you that, *cherie*. Look what he gave me." He held out his hand and at first all she saw was that his fingernails and cuticles were bloodstained again. Then she looked in his hand, where he was holding a plastic bag containing brick-colored powder.

Omar's right, she thought. It is some kind of drug business.

"It's salt. Red salt from Hawaii. Of course no one here is going to buy it, because they hate anything new. But it looks like Cajun red pepper salt. And Eggle assures me that it is an excellent salt."

Chancy picked up the little red and yellow plastic bag and examined it. It said on it "Alaea Sea Salt." And it did seem to be from Hawaii. It was not anything you could pick up around Worm Town. He had met with Eggle. This was exactly the sort of gourmet thing Eggle would have.

"Eggle and I are going to do another restaurant in Hawaii. I'm going to start flying there for meetings."

Then she realized that Andy had tricked her again.

"Andy, half the town has seen you coming out of the bayou covered with blood. People are getting really upset."

Chancy looked at the tall and somber Andy Ledoux and realized that she had never seen him smiling before.

"What?"

"It's the boudin."

"What?"

"The boudin rouge. I'm making boudin rouge. The French say boudin noir. It's rouge until you cook it and then it turns black. But it's illegal in Louisiana. They always had boudin rouge around carnival time and the old people love it. They expect it. It's not right to them to have a winter with no boudin rouge. It's like a winter without cold." He stopped for a second. "Well, some things we can help and some we can't. Tricky stuff, that blood. Somebody died from some blood that had turned and they banned it. That's why you do it in the wintertime. It's only dangerous in warm weather. Not that there's any cold weather this winter. But I'm careful and people expect it." He shrugged and looked at Chancy.

"Oh, Andy, for God's sake," she said angrily.

"You see, you've got to make it with fresh blood. You got to make it when the blood is still bright as pomegranate and pumping out of the pig. If I started bringing live pigs around here, I'd get caught by the health authorities. So we take the pig down to the bayou and stick a knife through its fat little throat and hold it over a bucket. At first the thing squeals something awful. That's another reason why you have to do it away somewhere. And if there are any dogs around, dogs make an awful fuss. Dogs can't stand it when you're sticking a pig. They know what's up before the pig does."

"Andy! What in the hell are you talking about!" She was determined that he stop making up these wild stories that no one was going to believe.

"The pig, *cherie*. I'm telling you about the pig. The pig

doesn't struggle until you stick it. But then, oh, man. Pig's a pretty big animal. Fights pretty hard and snorts and howls but by the time the bucket is half full it's not fighting anymore. You sauté some onions, a lot of salt, some cayenne pepper, thicken it over heat, add rice, and into the casings. Then I tie them off and bring them back here and boil them in a pot. That's the hardest part because they'll bump into each other and break, so you put lots of leaves in the pot to cushion them, and then . . ."

"Jeez, Andy," said Chancy. "Don't you ever stop?" And she ran out and ran home and cried and didn't tell anyone about the half-mad conversation she had had with Andy Ledoux about sticking pigs.

That night Andy went down into the bayou and Petey, after selecting a good piece from his woodpile, which he was not using this winter because it was too warm for a fire, followed after him, getting angrier every time he sank in mud or tripped on a root. But in the morning Petey came out, with only a little blood splattered on his blue work shirt, and Andy was nowhere to be seen.

It was almost noon when Andy emerged from the bayou, his face swollen and bleeding, blood encrusted around his nose and mouth and a cut above his right eyebrow. The blood had poured onto his white apron. He staggered and stumbled and called out, "Isn't someone going to help me?" It was late enough in the morning so that people were driving and walking by. They had all heard about how Andy Ledoux emerged from the bayou every morning, blood soaked. And there he was. They were not going to get involved with this. If it wasn't for the new traffic light, they would not even have slowed down.

Andy Ledoux closed his shop and left town. He said he was going to Hawaii to open a restaurant with Robert Eggle. No one believed him, but no one questioned it. Only Chancy ever thought much about him and she never discussed the subject. She didn't believe his Robert Eggle story either. Still, where did he get that red Hawaiian salt? She saved the bag just to keep the question mark. It reminded her that he might have been real and she hoped that would keep her from the inevitable—marrying someone like Petey Michoux. That was all that was left.

When anyone else talked of Andy Ledoux all they ever said was that he had made the best andouilles and hams. That was what they remembered. In the long run that was what people cared about in Worm Town. And at carnival time there was no more boudin rouge. A few people were sad about that too.

HOT POT

Gently she held his head in her hands and looked down tenderly at him, all of which was exactly the way he had imagined, but . . .

On every fact-finding trip he now took, Senator Green always kept himself open to the possibility of stumbling once again into the fondling touch of another Viridiana, a Hungarian Viridiana at the Budapest conference on global warming, a Peruvian Viridiana—not a stretch at all—at the Lima conference on overfishing, an Indian Viridiana at the Bombay conference on heavy metals. He was not a philanderer, he assured himself, and he loved Emma. Emma was exciting and unpredictable. But isn't it nice to fall occasionally into a quiet relationship? It might someday happen again, in a natural, unplanned way. He eyed assistants and translators with the greatest interest.

Then in China, in Chengdu, a two-hour flight from Beijing, the senator started getting that feeling again. The trip had started with a brontosaurus in the center of China that the scientists of the world, and more particularly of the United States, especially at a large university in his state, wanted preserved. The new capitalist, post-Maoist China wanted a theme park. It was a chance for a compromise— for a list of compromises—give up the brontosaurus but save the planet. They nodded so enthusiastically to everything he said that at times it seemed that they were not even waiting for the translation.

The translator seemed, he thought, perfection in black and white—ivory and onyx, like a keyboard. The hair a perfect black satin, the skin ivory, the eyes polished onyx. The few patches of her vanilla skin that he had seen registered in his hungry mind as sprawling fields of naked flesh—her face, her hands, a quick glimpse at the small of her back where her sweater once rose as she leaned to get into a car. Her full lips were painted red, the red of her sweater, a brilliant scarlet. The Chinese love red. Happiness. Brides marry in red. Does red, the senator wondered, mean sex the way it does in some cultures? Possibly not. Maybe they just worship red because they look so good in it. What else with ivory and black?

When her delicate ivory fingertips brushed his skin he had to admit he did not feel anything special. But he would be leaving soon and he did like to imagine peeling away the red wrapper. Would she cry out in Mandarin—or in English? Or in her local dialect? She was not from here. He did not know where she was from. He did not even know her name—a Chinese name with lots of vowels. It sounded to him something like "Oaouii." He couldn't remember their names. He knew that was disrespectful. He tried but he couldn't remember. And they were sometimes last name first, sometimes first name first. He didn't know which was which, nor, even if he did, whether he should call them by their first or last name.

Everything was upside down here. The senator briefly wondered if it was because it was the other side of the world. When the translator wrote out the addresses of his new Chinese partners, translating from their cards, the addresses began "People's Republic of China," and worked backwards to the name. To be lost in bed in an upside-down world on the other side of the planet—that appealed to the senator—as lost as you could get.

They all had business cards, which they presented to him with two hands and a small bow as though the card were something old and breakable. He had been warned that the card was important and had had his own printed specially, one side in Chinese and the other in English.

They had a problem with the name Green, finding an "ee" character. He could either be Senator Jacob Gren or Senator Jacob Lusè—the two-syllabled Chinese word for the color green. Sometimes he would hear them say the word "Lusè," even "Senator Lusè." And one of them, the one in the well-fitted dark suit, with silver hair, fine as corn silk, the one who had the Hong Kong contact, probably a Hong Kong suit, spoke a few words of English and he sometimes said "Gren."

They had all examined his card carefully, first looking quickly on the Chinese side, then studying the English side for a long time, as though fearful of a counterfeit—the Chinese are always wary of fakes—as though making sure he was really a westerner and not a Chinese tricking them.

Her skin seemed so perfect. Would she sweat during sex; would there be a soft sheen to what was now a lustrous matte finish? All he wanted was to be alone with her but he knew he could not propose that. So this was a farewell dinner. One in which he would somehow seduce her. There would be enough left of the evening after dinner because Chinese dinner meant five thirty, possibly because the Chinese can't wait to eat. Hard to seduce in daylight, he thought, and then wondered why that was, as though he were some kind of a vampire come to prey on China after dark.

"Maybe we could spend some time together after the

dinner?" he said awkwardly. But there was safety in ambiguity. She seemed to agree. About the ambiguity.

"We will have to see what happens after the hot pot," she said. What did that mean?

The Chinese had chosen a hot pot restaurant. He had eaten hot pot once in a Mongolian restaurant in New York. But this wasn't Mongolia; this was Sichuan. *La*, they called it, the burn of red peppers, like acid in the mouth. It was a stealthy poison. The first taste seemed harmless and then, seconds later, it would roll over the tongue like napalm. When he viewed the reddish liquid in the pot sunken into the center of the table, a few red peppers floating on the surface, he braced himself for pain.

The restaurant might have looked appropriate enough after nightfall, but in daylight it was clearly filthy. The floor was strewn with garbage and debris, slippery with grease. This made the senator happy. He was rarely in such a place. This was not like a state dinner. Or maybe it was, since it was a private room in an emptied restaurant filled with staff. Maybe this was where they had state dinners in Chengdu.

How gracefully she maneuvered her little red pumps through the grease, her exposed white porcelain toe with its red nail never brushing against the trash, while the senator, thinking of her delicate naked feet, slipped, almost fell on an oily patch. She held out her fine cream-colored hand to steady him. The restaurant was empty except for a staff member seated in a corner, noisily spitting on the floor behind his chair. The senator avoided looking at the translator because he could not seduce while others were spitting. The five were ushered into a private, windowless room—a little cleaner, but with no breeze. The stale air was pungent with spice; the fragrance of Sichuan red peppers fluttered in his nostrils, the light tickle that precedes pain.

The translator sat down softly, like an egret in a marsh, in the chair next to his—her place as his translator. The table was round and the other three were on the opposite side. Only in China does a round table have sides.

The one in the suit was named Cheng, or Chang. The senator wished he knew. Maybe Jing. The one next to him was extremely thin with long, thin, crooked teeth that showed on the frequent occasions that he smiled. The third one was the one who worried the senator. He had the Mao hairline, looked like a young Mao. Mao, it was said, seduced half the women in China. The senator calculated half of fifty percent of a population of one billion. Two hundred and fifty million women. Well, it would have been fewer if he did it when he was young, before the population boom.

This one, Senator Green reasoned, is out to do the same thing. And he will probably start, he thought, with my translator. Start? Surely he had already started. Were they looking at each other in a special way?

It seemed to the senator that all three, while trapped in a culture of modesty, were haunted by a suspicion of superiority—something they were too polite to express, possibly too superior to express. They wanted U.S. and international programs, so he was important. And yet the senator could not approach the level of their confidence. And the translator? A beautiful woman who does not display any knowledge of her own beauty. . . .

The long-toothed man lifted his glass of warm Sichuan beer and they all lifted their glasses of warm Sichuan beer—why didn't they chill the beer? The senator waited for the toast, bracing himself for the warm beer, waiting for his translator.

But the long-toothed one said nothing. Nobody spoke. They all just happily and eagerly clinked glasses. So the senator obligingly lifted his own glass and clinked each of the three of theirs and then turned to his translator to say a private toast, something in English. Suddenly, no English language toast came to mind. *Salud, santé, l'chaim.*

He had once heard a story about a diplomatic dinner in Mali. The Africans raised their glasses and, speaking French, said the French toast *tchin tchin.* The Chinese translator, thinking they had said the French word for China, "Chine Chine," translated "China China," and the head of the Chinese delegation responded, "Mali Mali." This would be a moment like that.

The moment passed. The translator had simply clinked his raised glass while the senator was thinking of his old diplomat's joke.

The waiter came in and kneeled beneath the table to adjust a gas hose that ran into the room and underneath the table. They were being gassed, the senator thought. And remembering the pain he had previously experienced from Sichuan food it occurred to him that gassing might be a preferable end.

The Chinese were preparing their bowls. The translator was doing his bowl. Hot peppers filled a third of the bowl and then it was mixed with salt, coriander leaf, and some other things, including MSG. The MSG worried the senator, but the peppers worried him more.

The waiter brought out a tray with chopped-up bony pieces of a large fish head and placed them in the pot, which was now bubbling. "Oh, I love fish head," said the senator involuntarily. He really did, the tender morsels between cartilage and bone, especially the cheeks and on the top, though it would be a challenge picking these parts out with chopsticks.

The translator smiled sweetly at him and translated into Chinese. The three laughed heartily. Did they think he was joking? Why had they ordered it if they thought he wouldn't like it? They raised their glasses again and they all clinked. This time he was able to look into the translator's shining black eyes as they clinked glasses and she smiled shyly. Her lips stayed slightly parted. The senator decided that he had somehow made contact. Finally, the first step. The fish head comment had worked. You never know what works in China.

The waiter was bringing out a dozen plates—sliced lotus, green leaves, two kinds of mushrooms, bean curd, smoked pork, green onions, thick bean flour noodles, thin rice noodles . . . delectable foods before they were put into the thick red liquor of the pot, now boiling ominously like a witch's brew.

They were all reaching into the pot with their sticks and pulling out pieces of fish head and placing them in their peppery little bowls. The senator did the same but quickly rescued the piece onto a small saucer before it became too infused with the mixture. Next he eyed a square of bean curd that had risen to the bubbling surface. Foolishly, he decided to try for it. A bean curd couldn't hurt you. But it fell apart under the crushing squeeze of his chopsticks and he retreated. The translator poked deep into the pot with her sticks and came up with a gently held piece of bean curd, which she placed in the senator's bowl.

She was looking after him. She regularly deposited pieces of fish head in his bowl because it was the star ingredient and because he had said he liked it. But she would occasionally treat him with a noodle or a vegetable. Was this good, the senator wondered? Or was this new relationship just fueling the Chinese suspicion that foreigners were inferior?

The senator had arrived at a strategy. He allowed a critical mass of foods to build up in his bowl so that the top pieces were not touching the peppery concoction at all. They were spicy enough and he was washing them down with warm beer. Periodically the Chinese would merrily insist on clinking glasses. Though he could not detect any alcohol in this beer, the senator noticed a gradual change in the demeanor of the three. Their posture loosened and he was almost certain that their incomprehensible speech was becoming slurred. Moist beads of sweat showed on their faces.

The translator, however, remained unchanged; her speech and bearing maintained their elegance, her matte skin its subtle luster. The senator thought that she probably would not sweat during sex. The thought of her sweating, of the perfect rendered a little imperfect, excited him.

But now his subterfuge, the food piled high in his bowl, was exposed. "No," she said. *"Bu bu bu,"* she entreated softly and the senator recognized the Chinese negative. She reached over and dunked his noodle in the red murk below. Panicking, he instinctively reached out and touched her hand to stop her. She did not seem to mind, as she moved her chopsticks, his hand in hers, and placed the reddened noodle in his mouth.

Was his mouth being torn out? A fire started on the back of his bruised tongue, spread to his swollen gums, stung his lips. He tried to smile at her through the pain and grabbed for his glass of beer. The three grabbed theirs and they were all required to clink before he could drink. But the beer didn't help; it just moved the oils around in his mouth, let them keep burning.

The translator signaled a waiter, who arrived with a bowl of rice. The rice soothed the senator's mouth and as he hungrily ate it, unable to get enough rice on his chopsticks, he thought he saw young Mao and the translator exchange a smile. But he had no time for this now. He had to continue his first aid.

The waiter came over and adjusted the gas valve somewhere near the senator's feet. The senator slowly regained his equilibrium, sat quietly, avoided eating. He started to realize that the high-hairlined one, the young Mao, was looking at him with condescension. Defiantly the senator resumed eating.

He longed to eat the raw green lettuce leaves, cool and crisp, before they were condemned to the hot pot. But he resisted, knowing how this would look to them, to him, to her.

She served him some green onions and some mushrooms. He obediently ate, smiling at her, trying to look confident, though he was aware that sweat was pouring down his face and she was not sweating at all.

Suddenly something, it seemed like a hot pepper, took a wrong turn down his windpipe. He coughed. He gasped. He wheezed, trying not to call attention to his predicament. The fire had moved down his throat. Soon it would be in his lungs. The pain sucked the oxygen out of his larynx. He was choking. He reached for his glass of beer and they all reached for theirs. Tears were running down both his cheeks. He could get no air. Through the distorted lens of tears he could see that they were smiling. Were they toasting him farewell? The senator waved his glass vaguely in their direction—it would have been unthinkable not to respond. Soon he would choke. He would die, collapsed on the filthy floor, additional detritus on the floor of a Chinese restaurant. A minor international incident.

The translator signaled the waiter and soon was caressing the senator's face with a steaming hot towel, her other hand gently cupping the back of his head the way she might support a baby's head while feeding it.

"Poor Senator Lusè," she said.

"Senator Gren," the English-speaking one corrected.

BELONS

elons? Belons?" Dave Harris, who now went by the name Jesse, announced—sounding like he was selling balloons—to the red-faced oyster shucker, who had no idea what he was saying but would have ignored him even if he knew. Inside Robo was behind the bar lifting a can of Orangina.

"Bonjour, bonjour," Dave said to Robo, apparently finding it more French to say everything twice. Robo pulled back his long silver and white hair, which, Dave had once pointed out, was the color of oyster shells. Dave thought a lot about oysters. His first great oyster experience had been many years ago when he had eaten them with Ernest

Hemingway. Now he was back in Paris. While this was just another night for Robo, Dave Harris was about to embark on his second great oyster experience.

The first time Dave Harris went to Paris there was a bustling all-night market in the center of the city, the parked cars were draped with fleshy prostitutes trying to look provocative in contrived poses, and the neighborhood offered dozens of cheap and dark restaurants where you could get a glass of harmless red wine for three francs, the sort of wine that tasted a little bit like rainy-day clay, and sip it all night. Harris could see that someone could live very well without much money in this neighborhood. That was what he vowed to do—someday—with a pension.

That day had finally come. He had changed his name to Jesse to announce the start of a new life. The restaurants were gone, the women were gone, and the market had been replaced by an underground shopping mall.

But Harris did not even notice most of this at first, because the restaurant where he had always gone was still there, still had cheap carafes of wine and oysters that were not so cheap anymore. The restaurant was in a building where four remaining fleshy women still did business. Others may have been put off by their age, but Harris liked thinking that these same women had probably been there when he first came and fell in love with the market neighborhood. They were something that had remained.

"Jezzay! Jezzay!" The ample women in the doorway called out to Harris by his new name. He didn't understand their nasal street French and they had no idea how to decipher what he called French. But he liked to chat with them because they were friendly; they laughed and joked with him and draped fleshy parts on him, nestled close, and smelled of alcohol and perfume. They were certain that he would take that walk up the stairs with one of them someday soon. Sometimes they thought that might be what he was saying and would start to lead him away.

He was able to rent, for very little money, an apartment with very little space, a *chambre de bonne* with barely enough room for a large mattress, which he put on the floor. The building was owned by the mother of a police officer, a colonel, which has three syllables and considerable authority in France. But he had no authority over his mother, who insisted on changing nothing in the building, including the rent. When the colonel was in his fifties he reasoned that his mother, in her seventies, would soon be gone and by then the neighborhood would be changed and his fortune assured. When the colonel was in his sixties, he reasoned that the values were climbing ever higher, and that his stubborn octogenarian mother would soon be leaving him a property worth a fortune. The colonel was now in his seventies and could barely bring himself to speak to his nonagenarian mother, who would change nothing. And so the increasingly decrepit building stubbornly remained in the increasingly fashionable neighborhood, with its inexpensive café and its inexpensive women.

By the time Harris finally came back to Paris, only this building was the same and, in truth, neither he nor Paris had changed entirely for the better. But he still had all his hair and no one had to know how old he really was—no one except himself.

"What an old geezer," he wheezed to himself, halfway up the six flights of stairs to the small *chambre de bonne* under the wet tin roof. The apartment was cold and damp, he could see his breath, and sometimes a stray mushroom grew behind the bathroom door, which, he reasoned, must be why the French called them *champignons de Paris*. One day when he found one he was so hungry he sautéed it on his hot plate and ate it with salt. Then he waited for the toxins to take hold. But it really was a normal mushroom.

He turned on the toaster that doubled as a space heater. Those few coils were all it took to heat this room. He found a crate that he used as a writing desk while sitting on the floor. He was back and he just hoped that no one would see how old he really was. After all, he didn't feel that old.

He had known Hemingway, though he seldom dared mention this because it sounded so ridiculous. He had met him once, anyway, which was all that was required to have "known" Hemingway. Harris looked up at the poster he had put on his wall with thumbtacks, his only decoration. He had bought it on the quay for three euros, which he thought of as cheap because he still thought in francs. Even the change in currency conspired to keep him from seeing how much Paris had changed.

The poster was an ad for oysters from Brittany, "Belons." Harris didn't exactly know what Belons were, but he had bought the poster because it advertised degustation all night and gave an address in Les Halles, the one-time market that was now a shopping mall.

The restaurant down-stairs was still cheap, if you didn't mind the difference between francs and euros. Three-franc wine was now three euros, which was more than fifteen francs, but Harris was not interested in such mathematical calculations. The restaurant was also a good place to bring what Harris called "visiting firemen," to show them the old Paris he was able to pretend was still there. He was going out with a visiting fireman tonight. Americans living in Paris had an endless

supply of visiting firemen, passing acquaintances from the States who wanted to have someone to look up when they took their trip to Paris. Visiting firemen did not want to spend a lot of money, but if you showed them something of Paris they usually picked up the check. Sometimes Harris could go for a week or two sustaining himself without spending one euro, whose value remained a mystery anyway, on food and only missing an occasional meal.

"Belons" Harris mispronounced with the "s." And he shrugged. He and Hemingway had eaten Portugaises—*Portugaises no. trois*, number threes. "Oh, man, were they good." So good he almost whined when he said it now. With Sancerre, which Hemingway ordered as he later wrote that he did. They had both published stories. Both of them. Hemingway and Harris, in the same issue of the same magazine. It was Harris's third story. "Damn fine," Hemingway had said. Hemingway had liked the word "fine." But no one believed this kind of story so Harris avoided telling it. But he often thought about it, because that fine story, his third, was also his last. The money ran out, he went back and got a job, and it all stopped. It didn't seem as bad at the time. Even Hemingway wasn't living in Paris anymore. But Harris stopped writing. Those Portugaises had been good, though. He remembered that. Almost shocking in their brininess, they tasted like the smell of a New England town at low tide.

. . .

"Bonjour, bonjour," he said to Robo at the bar. Robo pointed across the dark and musty room to the silhouette of Eric Krauss, the anthropologist, waving his arm at Harris with excitement. Even in the bad lighting, Harris could see the excitement from across the room. Robo was busy at the bar talking to a young woman whose face was concealed by a thick wave of dark hair.

Harris was disappointed because Robo was an interesting neighborhood character and talking to him was one of the reasons he liked the bar and he liked to show him off to visiting firemen. Robo had lived in California and spoke very good, almost American English, which was how Harris liked his Frenchmen. Often they had had great late-night talks about the 1968 uprising in the streets and the left and the right and winemaking and other very French subjects. Robo stood there until at least four in the morning. But it was clear that at the moment he just wanted to talk to this young woman.

"Dave!" said Eric Krauss, the excited fireman, and Harris cringed.

"It's Jesse now."

"Jesse? Why Jesse?"

Harris pointed toward the bar. "Did you meet Robo? He used to be a winemaker. He's from Bordeaux. Knows everything about wine. But he's always drinking orange soda."

"Really," said Krauss with concern. "There are people like that in the Northwest."

"Winemakers?"

"No. But people caught between their old culture and the new. Why are you Jesse?"

Why did he have to explain? "Should we get some oysters?"

"Sure, and I suppose it's Bordeaux here. We could get a Graves, maybe."

"Sancerre."

"That's Loire."

"Is it really? Robo won't care. I always like Sancerre." He thought of telling Krauss his Hemingway story but decided against it. "A long time ago, I had a writer friend—one of those people who had a way of knowing things—and he taught me that Sancerre was the best wine for oysters."

"Look," said Krauss, pointing at a small blackboard. "They have Belons."

"Belons, I'll be. That's what I asked the shucker outside. But he wouldn't tell me. The French always want to keep their secrets, you see. I have a poster of Belons in my apartment. But they are double the price of Portugaises. Portugaises are a fine oyster. Number three is a fine size."

"No, nothing like a Belon. You know what they say."

"What do they say?"

"The best aphrodisiac."

"Isn't that true of all oysters?"

Krauss shook his head in the negative, a gesture redolent of professorial knowledge. "They are two families. The crassostreas and the ostreas. They reproduce differently, which means they have a different sex life. The ostreas carry their young. It's ostreas you want. Men try to improve on crassostreas, but it's like powdered rhino horn. Don't believe it. But ostreas are the real thing."

"Well, I'll be. That's . . . that's wonderful. Just wonderful!" Kraus was still shouting, apparently excited about his information or maybe just about being in Paris.

"There is one ostrea in the Pacific Northwest, the Olympia oyster, and indigenous people value it above all the others, though, of course, it is *Ostrea lurida*, not *edulis*, but an ostrea nonetheless. And Belons are ostreas."

"Damn!" said Harris. Krauss knew everything. Especially about the Pacific Northwest. He even spoke some of their languages. Apparently he also knew a lot about oysters.

"Just tell them you want their best oysters and see what we get. Don't worry about the price. It's on me. Bottle of Sancerre and your best oysters."

Bottle? Harris could not help worrying that if Krauss went on like this when he was stone sober, what was conversation with him going to be like after a full bottle of Sancerre? No one ever ordered wine by the bottle in Robo's. What the hell, he said to himself. Visiting firemen.... *"Robo? Quelle est* the *meilleur* oysters?*"*

Robo looked at the woman with whom he had been intensely conversing and pointed at Harris and said in a low voice, *"Chancy, le client s'intéresse des huîtres."*

The woman turned to Harris and smiled, bringing out the fine architecture of her cheekbones. Her eyes seemed to glow a gold-flecked leaf green like maple leaves in late September. The beauty of her face, revealed so suddenly, had the effect of an almost blinding bright light. In her glow Harris vainly searched for particles of the French language, but found few. *"Bonjour, Madame.* I'm—*appelle Dave—acchhh—Jesse. Je suis Jesse. Je m'app . . ."*

She took his hand and held it in that same soft, inviting way that the women in the building had. "Hello, Jesse," she said in a slow, voluptuous voice but in a very American accent. "You wanted some oysters." She was still smiling as though there were some great joke that only Harris and she shared.

"Yes. *Quelle est le meilleur?"*

"Ahh, *le meilleur meilleur* are the Belons. You know what they say about Belons?"

Harris tried out what he thought was an innocent-looking smile. "No. What do they say?"

"I'll show you." She walked outside, almost a tease, as though she was threatening to disappear from his life forever. But she was just going to the stand where the red-faced man in an apron stood all night with a stubby knife in his right hand and never stopped prying open bivalves, which he tossed onto a bed of blue-gray crushed ice in front of him. She picked up a very round, flat oyster in her right hand, walked back in, placed her left hand under Harris's chin, and held the oyster to his mouth. Obediently, like a bird being fed, he opened his mouth and struggled to get his lips over the wide round shell and noisely sucked out the soft wet flesh.

On the one hand, he found this one of the most intimate contacts he had ever had with a woman in public and at the same time the oyster revealed itself to his taste buds with shocking salty intensity, a reduction of a thousand miles of seawater, a mountain of algae all concentrated into one half-liquid sip of flesh. He felt himself nearly overwhelmed with longing for this woman whose name he could not quite remember.

"Comment vous app . . ."

"Chancy," she quickly said, sparing them both any more of his French. "And I'm American. From Louisiana."

"Is that right!"

"You like the Belons."

"Oui!"

She started laughing. "You like them very much. You want to start with two dozen?"

He had never eaten more than six oysters in a sitting. *"Oui, pourquoi* not. And a *bouteille* of Sancerre."

Chancy gave an extra laugh for the wine.

Into the second dozen oysters and also halfway finished with the Sancerre, Harris and Krauss showed signs of slowing down. Krauss was talking about some Indian woman in Alaska and Harris was sitting quietly. Suddenly, as if he had not been listening to his own story, Krauss said, "God, that woman has a gorgeous face."

Harris, who was already staring in Chancy's direction, added in a determined tone, "And buttocks."

"What?"

"Come on, man, are those not the most glorious buttocks you have ever beheld?"

Krauss had to admit that they were, curved and shining in black leather pants that fit like skin. "Buttocks? Who calls them buttocks?"

Harris didn't know why he had said it like that. That wasn't his normal way of talking and he was feeling a little embarrassed. So he ate another Belon. "You know, Eric, you know when the last time was that I ate oysters this good? You know who I was with?"

"And breasts. My God!"

"Yes." Harris didn't want to talk about it anymore.

When Krauss had had his fill of his Paris evening it was only past midnight. Harris ran up his six flights of stairs, not in any particular hurry, but because he just felt like running. He couldn't sleep. He tried to read Orwell; he tried to read Stendhal; he tried to read . . . He knew what he wanted to do. He skipped down the stairs and walked up to the most gentle looking of the large working women, who was drooping on the fender of a parked car, festive as a balloon at a used car sale, and gave her some euros, the value of which he had no idea.

Robo gave him credit so that he could eat Belons every night; Chancy always smiled as she served them. Harris thought it was a knowing kind of smile. Did she know about the Belons? She had almost said it that first night. Then she must know what he was capable of. That must be an attractive thing to know. But still he didn't dare. He would come in and she would be in her place at the bar engrossed in conversation with Robo. He always came in late and there were not many customers. She would slip away from Robo and come to the back where he now always sat. He saw her as slipping away from Robo to come to him. Sometimes she sat down with him for a minute or two. Once she playfully ate one of his oysters.

Robo gave him credit for the oysters and wine, though he went back to his formerly three-franc *quart rouge*. His pension only went so far. But the women in his building would give no credit.

He tried to remember the expression—necessity is the mother of satisfaction? Realism mothers satisfaction? He couldn't remember but he no longer needed credit from the ample mothers of satisfaction. With his new oyster courage he was able to steer his flirtation with the Vietnamese laundress to his bed—several different nights. Then he met a German student who was subleasing the apartment on the fifth floor. She was not really very attractive but she was young and she had stamina and, miraculously, he was up to the job or, at least, she seemed to act as though he was. This gave him the confidence to bring home the American schoolteacher he met watching a juggler in front of the Centre Pompidou. She taught creative writing at a better school than he had and spoke much better French than he and was young enough to be his daughter though some people would have called her old. Now there was a terrifying thought that he got rid of as quickly as he could. She was older than the German but younger than the laundress. Probably any of them would be shocked to know his age. Only a little loose skin around his neck threatened to give him away. Someday he might have to resort to impressing one of them with his Hemingway story.

But for now, at an age he would not even admit to, he had become the man he had always wanted to be. He became a nocturnal predator. This seemed nothing short of an act of God. His first stop was always Robo's for Belons, and this he had to do by himself—whether to keep the oysters a secret or keep the women a secret he wasn't sure. The red-faced man with the knife was always at his station, never talked, never acknowledged him with more than a stare as though angry that Harris caused him to have to open that many more shells.

Harris knew where all this was leading. Gradually he was building back his confidence and possibly his testosterone until he was ready for Chancy.

When he walked in, Chancy and Robo were not having their usual conversation. Their faces looked angry and their voices sibilant as though they were trying to whisper but they were actually speaking very loud . . . but in French.

Neither said anything to him so he took his place in the back and in time she found him, her perfect cheekbones looking a little flushed, her green eyes bright. She seemed very happy to see him. "Belons, I suppose," she said and she practically winked at him when she said it.

"Why don't you sit here and have some with me?"

"That is an excellent idea," she said, and she walked out of the bar, giving him a view of her wondrous backside. Was she leaving or ordering the oysters? Would she come back? Would she just deliver them? Or would she actually sit down with him?

The long minutes passed and she came back with a dripping, icy tray that she put in front of him . . . then she sat down on the chair next to his and picked up an oyster, separated it from the shell with an oyster fork, and seemed to extend a long tongue and clear out the shell.

"You know," she said with a cryptic look in her eyes, "you are right to choose Belons. I grew up with oysters and there is nothing like a Belon."

"In Louisiana?"

"Yes, the bayous are full of oysters. But they are not Belons."

They sat and ate oysters and smiled and laughed and Harris tried to think of what to say next. Finally he said, "You know, I once ate oysters with Ernest Hemingway. Not Belons. Portugaises. Number *trois*."

Chancy leaned forward, her face very close to his as though trying to get a better look. "Ernest Hemingway?"

"Yes."

"The writer."

"Yes, we had both had stories published in the same magazine. . . ." But he saw a look of disappointment on her face.

"I cannot believe you are old enough to have known Ernest Hemingway," she said teasingly.

He felt something leave him.

"Were you and Ernest close?" she said. Before he could answer, possibly to stop him from answering, she said, "I have something for you." Chancy stood up and went into a dark and distant room. She came back with something in her hand and placed it in front of Harris. It was a small plastic bag full of a brick red powder.

"What is it?" Harris said with a feeble smile.

"It is something that was given to me. I thought it would give me good luck, but it hasn't," she said. "You take it. Maybe it will work for you. The person who gave it to me told me that he also had eaten oysters with Hemingway." She got up to leave and leaned close to him. "And he knew many other interesting people also." And she gave him a gentle kiss on his cheek.

A kiss on the cheek is never a welcome sign. Instead it was a night for the German, the last one, she told him, because she was going back to Düsseldorf.

When he went back to Robo's the following night he thought that something in the red-eyed stare of the oyster shucker was even more harsh than usual. He walked in and Robo behind the bar greeted him. He did not see Chancy but took his place in the back and patiently waited. After some time Robo shouted across the dark room, "Jesse. Belons and a *quart rouge*?"

"Where is Chancy?"

Robo responded with a Gallic shrug—the lips thrust out in an almost kiss and the hands up, displaying palms. The meaning is unknown, which in fact is what it means.

Chancy was never again seen in the restaurant; the German went back to Düsseldorf; the laundress and Harris got tired of each other; the working women, Harris came to understand, he could not afford. The Belons, which he also could not afford, did not seem to work anymore and Harris concluded that this was just as well. It was no life for a man his age. Krauss came back to town and wanted to go for more Belons but Harris didn't want them. "You remember that waitress?"

Krauss shrugged. Incredibly, he had no memory of her. Only of the oysters. "Look what she gave me," said Harris, and he showed Krauss the bag of red powder. A strange man, Krauss seemed more interested in the powder than he had been in the woman who gave it. "It's salt, you know," he explained. "But terrible eating. Captain Cook complained about the taste. The Polynesians only used it for their rituals."

"Here, take it," said Harris and he placed it in the other man's hand. Then they circled the mall where the market had been. Harris tried to remember where that first oyster place had been. Soon Robo's would be gone too. Paris really wasn't the same anymore. Neither was Harris.

MARGARET

You know you are on the edge when you live in Seattle, with nothing more to the continent than Puget Sound. The sound looks like a white-gray sheet of aluminum, often stained slightly darker by ripples of rain, as though the rain had gotten the water wet. On the opposite shore, icy peaks like unflavored gumdrops top the black ridges that float above the mist—the mountain range that is the last barrier before falling into the Pacific Ocean. The edge of the continent is as black and white as an old movie. If it were true, as was once believed, that you could fall off the edge of the world and be devoured by a giant turtle, Seattle would be a place where that might happen.

For Asians, Seattle is a place for their first step on

a different hemisphere, a new beginning, but for North Americans who move here, there is a sense that this is a place where people end up, and if you gave it enough time, just about all of humanity would drift into these mountains and you would see everyone you ever knew clinging to them in a last desperate struggle not to fall off the continent.

All Margaret wanted was a place where Robert Eggle definitely did not have a restaurant anymore. She was starting a business distributing Pacific Northwest wines and did not want to hear Robert Eggle's opinion of the pinot noir. She found a comfortable hilltop neighborhood, Beacon Hill, safely away from the sound, which seemed to her both menacingly finite and inexplicably expensive. On her more reasonably priced hill, she found an apartment with views on the top floor of a four-story building with a wooden fire escape, freshly painted white, running up the back. The bedroom was in a corner and the day she went to look at it, she could see Mount Rainier, snow covered, rising out of distant greenery. But then the winter rains set in and she never saw it again, as if it were some sleight of hand performed by the landlord to get her to move in.

On the floor below her lived a very small black man. There was something odd about the way he looked. Below him was the landlord and his wife, a large woman who constantly, and apparently futilely, exercised. On the ground floor was a young, very attractive Italian named Sandro, who had soft, amber-colored Italian eyes, wore sweaters of Italian lamb's wool, and spoke in an Italian accent. "Doesn't everybody just love Italians?" Margaret often murmured to herself.

"Buon giorno," Margaret would call to Sandro as he ran for his door carrying bags full of wiring and God knows what else—was he some kind of engineer? An Italian engineer?

"Oh, hello," he would say with that accent, trying not to show his amber eyes—was he shy? He would fumble for his keys and slip behind his door as quickly as possible, leaving only small puddles of rainwater that had run off him on the floor as proof that he had once stood there.

It was too bad he was so shy, Margaret would think. Maybe he just did not understand much English. Margaret had always wanted to take Italian lessons.

The landlord on the next floor up, like Margaret, was from New York. His name was Kugelman. It was Kugelman's wife who had wanted to move to Seattle. After the tech stocks collapsed she had an idea that there would be "bargains to pick up in Seattle."

Buying the Beacon Hill house as an investment had been Kugelman's idea. They had felt so disillusioned after the debacle of the Green presidential campaign. They were so close to having a Jewish president, when he was destroyed by such a little scandal. Kugelman failed to see how his sex life was anyone else's business. It seemed to

Kugelman it was just something dug up by anti-Semites. And that shiksa wife of his looked angry. Sure, she posed by his side but Kugelman and everyone else could see that they wouldn't stay together. That's what he got for marrying a shiksa, Kugelman thought. Kugelman's wife, Rogers, agreed (at least she had converted).

It was time for a change—which, ironically, had also been the slogan of the Green for President campaign—and Seattle, given its investment opportunities, seemed ideal even though it seemed a little white to Kugelman. But at least his building had some diversity, although no Jews, of course. Where would he find Jews here?

The top floor was the last one to be taken because the views justified a higher rent.. The first and third floors had gone quickly. Kugelman was a little bit proud of having rented to a black man. A lot of landlords would have turned him down. But the man was a wood-carver. And he had a local woman with a Seattle store that signed for him. He could tell the man had had bad experiences. He was probably from the South. When Kugelman gave him the lease and asked him when he was moving in he showed two greenish sticks about six inches long and said he was ready. The man had nothing. But he paid his rent. Kugelman was pleased with his little household, though he was a bit distrustful of the woman on the top floor. Something about the way she patted her lips was suggestive of anti-Semitism. But it was nothing that he could be sure of and she was the only one he found willing to pay the high rent for the top floor. Rogers, his wife, didn't like her either, hated the way she would call her Mrs. Kugelman.

"Rogers," she always muttered back but no one could make out what she was saying.

"Buon giorno, signor ingegnere," Margaret tossed out, trapping Sandro at last as he tried to make his way to his apartment with a large bag.

Sandro, with no place to hide, smiled. "I speak English," he said.

"Oh, so you do." She looked into his eyes. Was that hazel? It was a very special hazel. She could see that she was having an effect on him though she did not judge that to be a great accomplishment, he being Italian. She held out her hand in what was calculated to be a soft, sensuous gesture. "I am Margaret."

Sandro reached awkwardly with the hand that was holding his wet bundle. "Do you want to . . ."

Margaret knew exactly what he was going to say. He was going to invite her to get an espresso. How Italian! But unfortunately as he reached for her hand he dropped his package. The soggy brown paper split and she could read part of a blue label. Something about fertilizer.

"Oh, careful," came a booming voice from a dark little man. It was the man who lived underneath her and he was struggling to carry two very large bags of potting soil. Strange she thought, one with soil, the other with fertilizer. It seemed as soon as you left New York, you were living on the farm.

"Careful, careful," he said as he laid down his load and looked up at Margaret. "Hello, Lady," he said cheerfully. "My name is Joe."

He was not American. He had some kind of accent and for some reason Margaret was certain that his name was not Joe.

"Margaret," Margaret said with reluctance.

"Hello, Margaret Lady!"

Margaret had the clear sensation that this man was staring at her breasts. True, they were exactly at his eye level, but he could look up at her face, couldn't he? With his eyes trained straight ahead, Joe struggled with his fingers to extract something from the pocket of his blue jeans, which were several sizes too large for him. He handed it to her and she looked at it—two small reddish green leaves and a small orange, white, and gray feather, possibly from some kind of finch, all bound together with grass.

"Bye-bye, Margaret Lady," he said cheerfully and he picked up his soil and went up the stairs. "Joe, I am Joe!" And he was gone.

She turned to the Italian, who she remembered still had

not given his name—but he had gone. He had gathered his fertilizer and slipped into his apartment. She looked at his closed door and the puddles of water that showed the outline of his no doubt Italian shoes, then angrily threw the leaf and feather bundle to the floor but it would not even give her the satisfaction of smacking the ground; instead it drifted gently downward.

Joe seemed to brighten each time he saw her or her breasts, which he seemed to be smiling at. She often ran into him dragging bags of potting soil, raindrops perched precariously in his thick hair. She never saw the Italian. The person she always saw was Mrs. Kugelman, an unpleasant woman who mumbled under her breath whenever she greeted her.

But there was someone else of interest. A tweedy, cuddly, pipe-smoking kind of man. Actually she never saw him with a pipe. Unfortunately she did see him with a woman. The two of them regularly visited Joe.

The woman was the type that always irritated Margaret. She was fat and she didn't care. Not obesely fat but soft and jiggly everywhere. At least Mrs. Kugelman was trying. Actually the extent of the problem was not known, concealed by a tent of a dress in exotically patterned fabrics. And she did not even dye her hair but let her long gray locks flow down. She wore large earrings. She was the sort of woman who looked good in large jewelry. She was the sort of woman who looked good no matter what she did, even when she got fat.

But then Margaret saw something encouraging. The cuddly tweedy man and the large earringed woman were saying good-bye one evening in front of the building and they shook hands. The next time she saw the cuddly tweedy man, he was standing in the hallway by Joe's door. Margaret had just come in out of the rain and her hair was wet. She took off her jacket to show her moss green dress with the open back. Margaret had always regarded her back as her best feature—that long trough up the center and the nicely curved sides, shapely but without any fat. She shook her head and a few raindrops landed on the curved planes and she knew they would cling and then run slightly as she walked past him, the muscles of her body slightly undulating the skin of her perfect rear view.

She could feel his eyes on her, perhaps admiring the glistening raindrops.

"Hello, Margaret Lady!" came the cry from the doorway and she decided to keep climbing the stairs. Three minutes later he was knocking on her door. Amazing. She didn't like to say it but she just had a great back!

"Hello, Margaret?" he said.

"Yes?"

"Dr. Eric Krauss."

The cuddly tweedy man was a doctor?

"I was wondering why you were so rude to Joe down there. That man is very sensitive and you insulted him."

Margaret was stunned. She wanted to explain that she didn't like the way he looked at her but men never understand these things. He was probably looking at her the same way but just not when she could see it. So all she said was, "What is with the potting soil?"

"He likes plants. He comes from a forest and he misses them."

"It's not that he's black, I just . . ."

"He's not black."

"What is he?" she said, adjusting the collar of his tweed jacket. He didn't mind.

"We are not exactly sure."

He didn't mind! "You and that woman?" she asked lightly, dusting his shoulder.

"He works for her. He carves masks from the Pacific Northwest. He is a wonderful carver and she has taught him how to do masks. She had an idea that he was Polynesian. She has this idea that the Northwest culture and the Polynesian are related. She called me. I am an anthropologist."

He wasn't a doctor. And he didn't mind being straightened a little!

"But Joe's not Polynesian either."

"And his name's not Joe, right?"

"I think that's right. Look." He reached into his tweed

pocket and his hand came out with a card. "If you ever need to reach me."

Yes, this was good. Exchange cards. She opened her purse to look for hers and found . . . what was it? It was another three leaves and a salmon-colored feather bound together. How did he get in her purse? She angrily tossed it on a walnut sideboard near the door.

"Excuse me," Krauss said, pushing his way into her apartment, though he didn't think of it in that way. "Did he give this to you?"

"How did he get it in my purse?" Margaret demanded.

"I don't know," Dr. Krauss said in a wounded tone.

"I'm sorry. Would you have a drink?"

He readily agreed to a scotch. She took out a single malt, a sixteen-year-old Lagavulin. "Do you take it neat?" she asserted, making clear that he couldn't have it any other way. She didn't want to be that way but it was sixteen years old, and she wasn't going to put ice in it.

"So where is Joe from?" Margaret asked as they settled in the living room.

"He said he was a Tlingit, but he clearly isn't. I think he is Miyanmin." Krauss waited for a reaction.

"Where is that?"

"It's Papua New Guinea. In the mountains in the interior. Even on New Guinea you don't run into the Miyanmin unless you look for them. What I can't figure out is how he got here. About a year ago he started bringing his carvings to a downtown gallery. They were remarkable. But the odd thing was that they came from a half dozen cultures. When he does Haida pieces he is very delicate and subtle like the Haida. Then he would show up with these Bella Coola moon masks that looked like statues. Then he'd show up with these very simple Nootka masks. Then there would be these delicate heron helmets with sprouting wings that seemed Kwakiutl. But everything is always very authentic."

"Maybe he's stealing them," suggested Margaret, malice not completely absent from her voice.

"She thought of that, but he was supplying so many, she would have heard about the thefts. And she thought maybe he was farming out the work. But she would have heard about that. And he has no inhibitions about letting people watch him work. He sometimes carves right in her gallery. He seems completely alone and without a home. She got him this apartment. His masks have started selling for a few thousand dollars. He looks friendly, but he is very distrustful. He is just beginning to talk to me. He told me he was Miyanmin."

"Do you think he's legal?"

Krauss shrugged. "Why are you so hostile to him?"

"He stares at me."

"He doesn't mean to. Maybe he has never seen a woman like you."

"What am I like?"

Beautiful, he wanted to say. But instead he said, "Urbane," a word that even he was uncertain about.

She tried to conceal her disappointment. Why are men always leering too much or not enough?

They talked for some time and then Krauss looked at his watch, announced that it was late, and headed for the door. At the door he took her hand and then she kissed him and he kissed her back and the floor and the walls shook so hard that the leaves and feather drifted off the table.

"What was that?"

She opened the door and they smelled smoke and heard shouting.

"Joe!" said Krauss. And he ran down the stairs.

A filmy layer of smoke was swirling in the hallway, trying to cling to surfaces but only sticking to the ceiling. There was no one on Joe's floor. So they went down another two flights, where Kugelman seemed to be waiting for them.

"Who are you?" Kugelman demanded distrustfully.

"Dr. Eric Krauss," Krauss said while extending a reassuring hand.

"Doctor! Who called a doctor?"

"It's all right. I work with . . ."

"All done," said Joe, smiling with his large cheeks. "All done."

"That was good thinking," said Kugelman as he turned to Krauss. "How do you put out a grease fire, Doctor?"

Krauss stared at him uncertainly.

"You throw earth on it."

"Yes," said Sandro, emerging from his smoky apartment with a look like he had just been caught at something. "Joe putta out de fire with the earth."

"Threw potting soil on it," said Kugelman. "Saved the day."

"Estupid me," said Sandro, slapping his forehead. "I try and-a make-a de pasta!" It seemed to Margaret that his accent had somehow gotten much more pronounced.

"*Scusate, scusate.*" And he shut the door.

Margaret looked at the triumphant Joe and, yes, he was staring at her breasts. "I suppose you just keep soil around in case there's a pasta fire?"

"No, Margaret Lady. Come, I show you." And he ran up the stairs with an agility she imagined could have been honed on steep tropical mountain paths. When Margaret and Krauss got to his landing Joe was already in his apartment. He called through the open door, "Come, Margaret. Come see." Cautiously she walked into the apartment, which was dark and . . . and empty. Krauss came too, even though uninvited. He had been there before but he had to see what Joe wanted to show Margaret. In the back corner bedroom was a hammock, a toy hammock—bubble gum pink with a baby blue picture of Donald Duck in the center, hanging from hooks in the wall. The floor was strewn with wood chips and shavings and along the far walls under the windows were wide, two-foot-high, five-foot-long wooden planters full of soil but containing only one plant in each. The plants were about five feet tall and had broad leaves that separated like a six-fingered, dark green hand. There were also smaller leaves, almost like chartreuse flowers covered with a shiny substance, or was it sticky?

Joe pointed at the two plants that were taller than him. Margaret thought about how everything conspired to make him look smaller—the big teeth, the tall but not very tall plants, the baggy blue jeans, the red and charcoal flannel shirt that was so big the shoulder seams were at his elbows. Joe reached into his shirt pocket and pulled something out that he held in his fingers. It was either a cockroach or some kind of beetle, and its little angular legs were still squirming. Joe placed the bug on one of the chartreuse leaves and it lay there motionless for a second. Then the leaf curled around it and it disappeared except for one leg, which Margaret thought she could still see sticking out on the side.

Margaret stared, her face demonstrating all the disgust she was feeling at this little man who smiled back—at her breasts. "You see, Margaret, my plant is good for our home, good for the building." He was still smiling.

Could she call Immigration and have the little bug man thrown out?

"Here, Margaret Lady. I have something for you." And he was gone to the next room and back only seconds later. Margaret realized that his footsteps made no noise. She looked down, expecting to see bare feet, but instead saw that he was wearing heavy workman's boots. His feet too were oversized and helped make the rest of him look small.

He was holding out a mask, a white face with red lips— a sad face full of yearning.

"For you," said Joe.

Margaret looked at Krauss, whose eyes said, You have to take it. She ran her long, thin fingers over the smooth surfaces of the fine carving.

"You made this? It's beautiful."

"It's for your apartment. It will be good . . . like the plant."

Margaret eyed him with suspicion.

The mask ended up in the hallway leading to her bathroom, hanging in her apartment nevertheless. Krauss explained that it was Pugwis, the ghost of a drowned fisherman who now lived under the water. But Margaret insisted that it was death pursuing her. "Don't you see, it's some kind of voodoo."

"I don't think Miyanmin practice voodoo," Krauss said. She flattened the left collar point on his shirt.

"They don't carve masks from the Pacific Northwest either. But there he is. Don't be the smart fucking college professor with me. This is serious. Don't you see how he has done everything he could to try to plant something of his in my apartment? It's about control. Power or something."

"I think he just likes you," Krauss said, but he was not certain that Margaret wasn't right. In any event, he pointed out, it would be bad luck to get rid of the thing, which made sense to Margaret. He also pointed out that it was worth at least two thousand dollars and that also made sense to Margaret.

Like her framed Bordeaux labels, like many things in an apartment, Pugwis was just there and was never looked at or thought about. For that matter her diminutive neighbor was seldom seen anymore in the hallways or on the glistening rainy Beacon Hill streets or even in her thoughts. She, after all, was busy trying to build a new business.

She had time for Krauss, though. He was cozy, when he wasn't being too pompous. She was making a new life here in Seattle, the moist and gray last stop. So was Mrs. Kugelman, who would jog by, grimacing.

But Joe thought Mrs. Kugelman was a pleasant woman. "Hello, Rotchers," he would say, without any idea what the word meant. And she would always smile back at him.

Margaret was in a deep sleep in her corner bedroom, sent off by the rhythmic tap of rain on the windows. Suddenly she had an odd feeling, as though someone was reaching out and trying to grab her. Instantly her eyes were open. The turquoise electric number on her clock said exactly

4:00 a.m. From off in the periphery she detected movement and gave out a little startled wheeze as she sucked in air. Out the window, on the fire escape, were hands reaching for her or reaching for the window or maybe they were just flailing with no particular purpose.

No, they were just leaves. Leaves on the fire escape? Why were there leaves on the fire escape? She opened the window. It was a vine, several of them, running up from below and continuing past her up the wooden railing. Soon they would reach the roof. She did not need to look down to know where they were coming from. He was sending his vine up to invade her apartment. To join Pugwis. To strangle her in her sleep. To grab her breasts. The vines were climbing to the roof. They would envelop the building, eat them all like bugs. This man was no innocent, she was sure of that. Not at all innocent.

She could see some kind of crushed wing in the grasp of one rolled-up chartreuse leaf. Another chartreuse leaf lay near the open window. She held out her finger and the leaf grabbed it and tried to wrap around it but she pulled away. She could still feel the stickiness. Had it grabbed her finger or had she reached out and touched it? She wasn't sure.

The next morning she stopped off at Joe's door and knocked. He answered, looking genuinely delighted to see her. "Hey, Margaret Lady, come in. Come, come." As she started to enter she could see in the morning light that his bedroom on the other side of the empty living room was becoming increasingly green, with vines now running on all the walls and dropping down from the ceiling.

"No, thank you," said Margaret. "I have no time. I just wanted to ask you to cut down the vine from the fire escape. It's starting to block the view from my window."

"Cut the vine? No. No, Margaret Lady. The vine is good."

So Margaret went to Kugelman and complained. But Kugelman said, "I don't see the harm. The vines will keep away the cockroaches."

"I haven't seen any cockroaches here."

"You see?"

As far as Kugelman was concerned, this woman was being difficult because she didn't like having a black man for a neighbor. He would have nothing to do with such racism. She was probably an anti-Semite too. That type always are. Besides, his wife didn't like her. She liked Joe. Kugelman trusted his wife's judgment. She had been right about the market.

Every time Margaret and Krauss made love in her bedroom, which was taking place with increasing frequency, sometimes even several times a day, Margaret's pleasure was diminished by a vague sense that she was being watched. She would imagine the sad and lonely white-faced Pugwis watching her, but he was now safely away in the linen closet by the bathroom. Then she would look out the window at the fire escape and laugh at herself. Why should she care if a plant wanted to watch? It was starting to look like a rain forest out there. Why didn't all of Seattle look like a rain forest, since it rained all the time? But every time she was making love, on the way to orgasm, she would give in to the urge to shoot a glance toward the fire escape.

One dawn on the way to achieving their third event of the night, Krauss behind her, Margaret facing the foot of the bed, she looked up at the window and there he was—Joe, in the rain forest. He was absolutely naked and Margaret could see that his penis, which was a strange whitish color, was yet another oversized part of his body designed to make the rest of him look smaller. She screamed. He was gone.

Krauss had seen him too and was annoyingly fascinated by what he saw. "What was he doing?"

"What do you think he was doing! He had an erection. He was watching us. I think he was masterbating!"

"I don't think so."

"Why don't you think so?" asked Margaret.

Krauss promised that he would talk to him. She insisted that she wanted to be there too, and when Kugelman saw the two of them marching to Joe's door, he decided he'd better follow. Kugelman could not help noticing their argument.

"It was a huge erection!" Margaret was saying.

"I don't think so."

Nearly in tears with frustration, Margaret turned to him. "Why don't you think so?"

"I don't think he had it out."

"It sure looked out to me."

"No, it was sheathed."

"Sheathed! What does that mean?"

"He was wearing a penis sheath. Some sort of gourd, I suppose."

"So that's better? He's standing outside our window jerking off and you think it's all right because he's got his prick stuck in some squash or something!"

"Is there a problem?" Kugelman asked.

"Yes, there's a problem," said Margaret. "I've got a Peeping Tom on my fire escape and I want this to stop! I'll call the police! I'll go to court!"

"Oh." Kugelman did not want anyone calling the police and he especially didn't want anyone going to court. He knocked on Joe's door.

"Hello, Boss. Hello, Docta. Hello, Lady," said the cheerful and fully clothed Joe, looking frail in his baggy flannel shirt. Margaret now knew how much sinew was concealed underneath.

"I'm sorry," said Kugelman, "but we've had a complaint."

Joe looked confused.

"Look," said Krauss, "I'm sorry but I saw you out there."

"Out the—," said Joe, pointing through his apartment to the back window. Margaret noticed that the vines had now left the bedroom and were climbing the living room walls and stretching across the floor, looking for a new room to conquer.

"Joe, you just can't do that." It occurred to Krauss that Joe might have little sense of privacy and the concept was going to be difficult to communicate. "People don't like being watched. Especially women don't like being watched . . . by men."

"Watched?"

"Through the window from the fire escape."

"Out there?" He pointed toward the window. "Watching you?"

"Yes," said Margaret. "Are you going to say you were not on the fire escape naked early this morning?"

Joe's smile returned. "Yes, out there! Yes!"

"Joe, what were you doing out there?" said Krauss in his headmaster voice.

"I went out to see God."

"What?" said an outraged Margaret.

"I'll show you." He led them through his apartment to the thick jungle with the hammock in the back, out the window, and up the fire escape. Fortunately the rain had stopped. They climbed and when they got to Margaret's floor Joe made a grand gesture outward and said, "God."

They all looked, and there it was. Margaret should have

seen it from her window but she hadn't been looking. The four of them stood in silence in the rich, warm morning light and there in the distance, rising out of a green forest, was Mount Rainier, powerful and graceful, refracted in lemons and pinks and violets in the moist sunlight, the earth artfully stretching up to the sky, an awesome, lovely, white-headed giant—God.

"Well," said Kugelman, breaking the silence. "I have work to do." He started down the fire escape.

Krauss was chuckling. "God," he said softly.

"God," Joe affirmed and Krauss nodded his head in agreement. Margaret stood there, feeling the frustration of having been outmaneuvered, while Krauss started to climb in her window.

"You know, Margaret Lady," said Joe in a quiet voice, almost a whisper, "you know in my people we learned that if you do *baliberi* like a people, it produces more children than when you do it like a buffalo."

Margaret screamed. Krauss came climbing back from the window. Margaret was pointing a long finger at him. "I am going to get you. I will find a way. I will call the goddamn INS."

Joe looked confused and turned to Krauss. "Who is the Ironess?"

"INS. The immigration people. If you entered the country illegally, they can throw you out."

And then Joe wore a face neither of them had ever seen

before, a serious and reflective face. Joe had just realized something important. He realized that Margaret was his enemy. This was important, because up until this moment, Joe had not found any enemies in Seattle and his survival was only assured if he had an enemy. He said in a quiet voice, *"Bokis es bilong mipela."*

"What?" said Krauss.

Joe pointed at Margaret. He was staring at her oddly, as though seeing her for the first time. *"Bokis es bilong mipela."*

Krauss struggled. "Bokiss . . . she is your . . . she is your . . . refrigerator? Or your pantry?"

Joe nodded.

"I am not," Margaret said with determination. "I will not allow him to store any food, or anything else, in my apartment."

"I don't think that's what he's saying," said Krauss cryptically, not wanting to make things any worse.

Krauss was trying to talk to Joe as much as he could, because Krauss was an anthropologist and Joe was what anthropologists call an "informant." It was not that Krauss wanted to know the ways of the Miyanmin, which was far away from his field. But he wanted to know how this Miyanmin got to Seattle and how he learned the traditional carving of the Pacific Northwest.

And what was this refrigerator business about? He was certain that it wasn't about refrigerators. He wanted to make amends for the incident with Margaret because Joe seemed upset. A gift was what was needed. What would be a gift for Joe? A carving knife? Krauss looked around his own apartment, which abounded in possibilities because Krauss saved everything from his research. There were carved bones and woven grass and an entire collection of throwaway cigarette lighters. Those were always popular. He had five different cheap watches with faces in bright colors. Those were also a good item. But then, next to a pile of different bright-colored bubble gums, he found just the thing.

Krauss went to Joe's apartment with a gift, a bag of Hawaiian red sea salt. He knew Polynesians used it for religion and hoped that Joe might value it as well. Joe looked at the bag; he opened it and took a few crystals delicately in his fingertips and dropped them on his tongue. Then he smiled. He said something that Krauss did not understand and threw some crystals on his floor. "Thank you, my friend," he said. And the hard look vanished and they could talk again.

Joe was constantly carving, digging a blade into wood, shaving surfaces. He carved in the gallery and he carved in his apartment. He talked of home, of his family, but not of how he happened to come to Seattle. He told Krauss of "the bad time." He dated things by it. This was "before the bad time." Or "since the bad time."

But what exactly, the increasingly frustrated Dr. Krauss wanted to know, was "the bad time"?

"It was a very bad time," Joe confirmed.

"What made it bad?"

Joe was rubbing a cedar mask with a cloth, bringing out the grain along the edges. The face itself was painted blue, with deep red lips.

"Was that why you left, because of the bad time?"

"No." Joe smiled. "Long after that. The bad time ended."

"How did it end?"

Joe carefully lifted the mask and hung it on a nail on his wall where he had parted the green vines that now twisted everywhere in all of his rooms.

"We ate."

"So the bad time was when your people did not have enough to eat?"

Joe nodded in agreement as he gently arranged the strips of cedar bark that served as hair for the mask.

"Where did you get the food?"

"We ate *bokis es bilong mipela.*"

Krauss leaned toward his informant. He was using that phrase again. "You ate from the refrigerator? The pantry? I don't understand."

"We ate our refrigerator."

Joe turned from the mask on the wall and glanced at Krauss and took pity on him. "It was a village."

"What was?"

"The refrigerator. They were our enemies."

It was clear that Joe did not want to talk anymore so Krauss left him to his carving. The next day he stopped by and found Joe putting finishing touches on the same mask and in a better mood. He chatted with him for some time before asking, "So you were saying that your enemies were a certain village and they were your refrigerator?"

"Yes," he said softly while buffing the wood and arranging the cedar hair. "They had been designated—in case we needed them. The bad time got so bad. It was during the wet season and the season never ended and there was nothing else to hunt. It took three weeks."

"What did?"

Joe continued carving but said nothing, and Krauss understood that this was all he wanted to say, possibly more than he wanted to say.

Some days later he was able to pick up the conversation again. "The village was a very hard place to get to. No one ever went there. That was why we picked them."

"I thought you picked them because they were your enemy."

"Yes," Joe said flatly. "We built bridges. Went in very quietly and we killed all of them."

This was incredible! Krauss wished he could take notes. "How many?"

Joe shrugged. "Maybe forty. We had to kill all of them

or the ones we left would get us later. Except the children. We kept some children. Very nice children." Joe smiled sweetly, thinking of the children.

Krauss was beginning to understand. A refrigerator for storing food. He felt enzymes eroding the lining of his stomach, a slow, uncomfortable feeling. He wanted to know more and he didn't want to know more. But this was enough for now.

The next time Joe explained how they were killed, with a downward thrust near the collarbone. He demonstrated with his carving knife, though the actual deed had been done with a sharpened bone.

The next day Krauss nervously chatted with Joe for a while and then said, "So the refrigerator village—you killed them, and then what?"

Joe explained while rubbing wood how the heads and limbs were cut off. The bodies were gutted. It was all packed up and taken with them, even a bag for the heads. His village ate well. "And when the meat was gone so were the rains." Joe smiled. "It wasn't very good," he added, as though this were a comforting thought.

Krauss looked through the vines at the clear and darkening night sky. It was not raining here anymore either. Joe showed him the sharpened bone, made from some kind of thigh bone, Krauss thought. He wondered if the dark brownish stains were blood.

"Shit!" The voice was at the door. Then a sound like a stamping foot. Krauss looked at the door, then at Joe. Joe didn't care who was at the door. He was admiring his mask, the blue-faced woman with the arranged cedar bark hair and the full red lips. He rubbed the face once more with the cloth and lightly patted the lips.

Suddenly Krauss realized—it was a mask of Margaret.

Sandro had not been fooled from the outset. One look at the tweedy Ivy League–looking man hanging about his building, talking to all his neighbors, and he could see that he was an agent of some kind. Probably FBI. And that friendly little black man who had put out his fire had turned informant. Running in with the sack of soil had been no more than a clever way to get in his apartment. He had probably reported everything to the tweedy man. But now he could not believe what they were talking about. Should he warn the woman? But who was she working for? She spent a lot of time with the FBI agent too. And those vines had reached out from under the little man's door and grabbed his shoelace.

It was evident to Sandro that the FBI was planning some unspeakable act, hiding heads in bags and who knew what else. Sandro realized that no one would believe him and that he alone could stop them. He began prowling the halls, listening to conversations. Why was the woman always so interested in talking to him? Was she reporting to the agent too? But this sort of thing worked in two directions. What could he learn by talking to her?

Margaret did not like Krauss always talking with the little man. And it had not escaped her that the Italian had started noticing her. Margaret and Sandro started having long talks in the hallway. Words seemed to flow from Margaret as though she were afraid that if she stopped talking he would disappear. What was she up to? Sandro could not understand her. For some reason she kept questioning him about the making of mozzarella cheese, about cow milk verses buffalo—were there different kinds of buffalo? Sandro, who knew nothing about cheese making, was convinced that in time he would learn something important if he kept talking to her.

"So have you found out what 'refrigerator' means?" she asked Krauss, tightening the knot on his tie.

"Yes," Krauss said. "It was a mistranslation. I made a mistake. He was calling you a goddess, admiring your beauty."

"That is so creepy!" Margaret protested. "I can't stand the way he looks at me. Like I'm an hors d'oeuvre."

"No," muttered Krauss. "I don't think Joe thinks about hors d'oeuvres."

"You see! Men just don't understand how creepy it is to be looked at like that."

"Margaret," said Krauss, "I do understand. I really do."

And he held her and then they made love and all the while she kept looking at the vines on the fire escape. She couldn't help it. When she made love she expected him to appear. She would have to get curtains—those thick blackout curtains that they had in hotels.

It was when Margaret started turning the conversation away from mozzarella and on to gelato that Sandro began to despair.

As she grilled him about the fat content and the storage temperature he concluded that this woman was not cunning, she was completely *pazza*—crazy. Instead he would turn his attention toward the FBI agent, who, the more he talked to him, the more Sandro began to suspect was actually CIA. For one thing, he claimed to be an anthropologist. That is a CIA cover. FBI agents rarely pass themselves off as anthropologists. Sandro lured him in by claiming to be a fellow academic with a doctorate in philosophy.

"Philosophy! From where?" Krauss seemed pleased by this information.

"Milano," said Sandro.

"What is your specialty?"

"Bakunin."

"Bakunin," Krauss repeated and Sandro thought that

this might be a mistake, so he quickly asked where he studied.

"In New Haven," said Krauss.

This was disappointing. CIA agents did not come from the University of New Haven. But later, in conversation, he came to realize that Krauss was lying to protect his cover, that actually, like most CIA agents, he had gone to Yale.

Sandro was elated by this discovery. He invited Krauss to come with him to a popular neighborhood espresso place with very bad espresso, though he alone seemed to notice this. It became an afternoon ritual, very much to the irritation of Margaret.

"*Buon giorno*, Sandro," said Margaret.

Sandro gave a weak "Hi." Even that syllable sounded a little sad to her. Why was he more interested in Krauss than in her? She gave her best walk up the stairs and could feel, with some satisfaction, the gaze of a man's eyes on her backside. But then Mrs. Kugelman in her jogging clothes slipped past Margaret going downstairs. Margaret said, "Hello, Mrs. Kugelman," and the woman just muttered something as she always did. As she passed, Margaret heard what she expected would be Sandro's voice. But it was Joe's.

"Hi, Rotchers!"

Joe couldn't help thinking that Rotchers was a far meat-ier, far better specimen than Margaret. But she smiled so nicely. It made him too sad to think about eating such a nice lady. He looked at skinny Margaret. The lady had com-plained that he was making more carvings than she could sell, that big money wasn't around in Seattle anymore and "things were slowing down." What did that mean? Joe wor-ried. For now, he had all the food he needed. He looked up at Margaret climbing the stairs. She had nothing. But she was as close as he had to an enemy in Seattle. She did have a little bit in the rump.

On the next landing, Margaret saw Kugelman. "Look at him," she whispered angrily. "He is just standing there staring at my butt!"

When she got to her own apartment, she saw a small object in front of her door. She bent over, first checking behind her that Joe was not there staring. It was three leaves and a pinkish feather neatly tied together with grass, propped up on some kind of little dirt mound. She angrily kicked it over and as she unlocked her door felt grit under her Italian leather shoes. She was about to walk in when an idea struck her. She looked down at her feet. Margaret touched a long, well-manicured index finger to the powder on the floor and brought it to her lips.

She recognized it immediately. Sea salt. Hawaiian red sea salt. And she patted her lips.

ACKNOWLEDGMENTS

Thanks to my agent, Charlotte Sheedy, and my wise and gracious publisher, Geoffrey Kloske. And to my friend and editor, Nancy Miller, who keeps me honest and makes me better with her persistent, annoying, and well-aimed questions. Thanks also to Virginia Peters Mann, who believed in the story many years ago before anyone else did. Thanks to Tim Flannery, the intrepid Australian, who told me about his experience with the Myanmin, and to my brother Paul and wife Helaine, whose cholent recipes were in some ways much scarier than Tim's tales from New Guinea.

Mark Kurlansky is the *New York Times* bestselling and James A. Beard Award–winning author of many books, including *Cod: A Biography of the Fish That Changed the World*; *Salt: A World History*; *1968: The Year That Rocked the World*; *The Big Oyster: History on the Half Shell*; *The Last Fish Tale: The Fate of the Atlantic and Survival in Gloucester, America's Oldest Fishing Port and Most Original Town*; *The Food of a Younger Land*; *The Eastern Stars*; and *Nonviolence: The History of a Dangerous Idea*; as well as the novel *Boogaloo on 2nd Avenue*. He is the winner of a *Bon Appétit* American Food and Entertaining Award for Food Writer of the Year and the Glenfiddich Food and Drink Award for Food Book of the Year, as well as a finalist for the *Los Angeles Times* Book Prize. He lives in New York City.

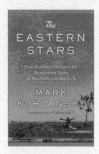

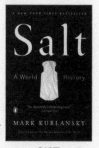